RENEGADE RANGE

RENEGADE RANGE

STEVEN GRAY

A Black Horse Western

ROBERT HALE · LONDON

© Steven Gray 1993
First published in Great Britain 1993

ISBN 0 7090 5139 5

Robert Hale Limited
Clerkenwell House
Clerkenwell Green
London EC1R 0HT

Photoset in North Wales by
Derek Doyle & Associates, Mold, Clwyd.
Printed in Great Britain by St Edmundsbury Press Limited
Bury St Edmunds, Suffolk and bound by
WBC Bookbinders Limited, Bridgend, Mid-Glamorgan.

ONE

Lester Peabody came to a halt outside the door of the stagecoach office. Tucson, Arizona, he thought, who needed it? Even this late in the year – Christmas was only a couple of weeks away – it was still hot, dusty and brown. He'd never liked Arizona. But he'd been summoned. It was where the work was. Perhaps, with luck, the job would be easy and soon over. Perhaps.

Pausing to wipe his shoes on the back of his trousers, he opened the door going into the office.

'Mr Thorndike is expecting you,' the clerk said, nodding towards the inner door. 'You're prompt anyhow.'

Being on time and reliable were Peabody's trade marks.

He'd met and worked for Edgar Thorndike a couple of times before. Thorndike knew Peabody's reputation wasn't exaggerated, which was why he'd sent for him again.

'Ah, Lester, good to see you. Sit down.' Thorndike was in his sixties and everything about him was grey: hair, beard, eyes and smart clothes, the only spot of colour a gold watchchain stretched across his ample paunch. He was the owner of the local stagecoach company that ran, when allowed to by Indians, weather and outlaws, from Tucson up to the Griffin Creek, and Fort Sherman, and then beyond to California.

For a moment or two the men exchanged pleasantries then anxious to get on to employer/ employee basis, Peabody said, 'What can I do for you, Mr Thorndike? Your message sounded urgent.'

Thorndike leaned back in the leather chair, which creaked beneath his weight, and frowned. 'It was urgent when I sent it. I'm not so sure now.'

'Oh?'

'A short while ago my line was robbed several times near Griffin Creek. You may have read about it?'

'I believe I did hear something. Bunch of ex-Rebs were responsible weren't they?'

Thorndike nodded. 'Crazy fools. Wouldn't you think they'd have had enough of fighting in the war? But no, no sooner had Lee surrendered than they got a damnfool notion about recruiting a new Southern army and starting it up all over again.' The man snorted in derision. 'There were five of 'em! Five! I'm not exactly sure what sort of battle they thought they could fight.'

Peabody grinned in sympathetic amusement. 'What indeed?'

'Even so, the bastards still did a lot of damage. Not only were a number of passengers robbed but one of my guards was shot and killed. With that, feelings started to run high against them. Then, for some reason, the gang fell out amongst themselves.'

'What happened?'

'I don't know the whys and wherefores, only the outcome. Which was that three of them were shot and killed over in Griffin Creek and the other two skedaddled. They haven't been heard of since.'

'There haven't been any more robberies?'

'No.'

'I'm sorry I couldn't get here any quicker. I was finishing off another job when your message reached me.'

Thorndike waved his hand. 'It wasn't your fault. I know that. You made your reasons for delay clear enough. I could always have hired someone else. I wanted to hire you.

'Am I too late?' Peabody hoped he wasn't. He disliked law-breakers, especially those who robbed innocent folk and killed someone for doing his duty.

'No, you're not. Even though they're unlikely to bother me again, I still want the two who got away. Just to let them go is bad for business. They stole from me and caused me several sleepness nights. The stage almost had to stop running. I had to tell the guard's wife her husband was dead and their children left without a father. The bastards can't be allowed to get away with it. If they're not caught and made an example of, there's the risk of others thinking they can do the same thing.'

Peabody agreed.

'Usual payment of course.'

Peabody agreed with that as well.

'I know it might be difficult. It was over a month now since these two disappeared.'

'I guess the best place to start will be Griffin Creek.'

'You could also drop by Fort Sherman. The soldiers had some sort of run in with them as well.'

'What are their names?'

'Harry Phillips and Jarrod Kilkline. My clerk has got their description.'

'Will I find them with one another?'

Thorndike shook his head. 'Way I heard it, they had a falling out.'

'Never mind.' Peabody got to his feet. 'I'll find them, no matter how long it takes.'

When Peabody left the stagecoach office and made his way back to the hotel, no one took any notice of him, except maybe to grin at his appearance.

Peabody was thirty-five, of middle height and slim build. His dark brown hair was slicked back with grease and he had a ruddy complexion. He was a natty dresser, wearing derby hat, vivid check suits with vests to match, and shoes.

Many Westerners he met considered him an Eastern greenhorn. That was how he liked it and it was their mistake. He knew the land and how to live on it better than most of them. He was good at tracking and while there was no revolver in a holster by his side, hidden about his body were various weapons of different kinds, all of which he was proficient in using.

There were times he thought of going back East to live; it wasn't as if he needed the money, he already had enough stashed away to open a store or buy a farm. That was the trouble. He couldn't see himself spending the rest of his life behind a counter or a plough – not when there was the excitement of the chase and the homing in on his prey.

He was good at what he did; and liked it too. Despite the hardships, uncertainties and dangers – or maybe because of them – he didn't want to give up. Not yet anyway.

Thorndike knew that once paid to be on the trail, Peabody wouldn't let go. The finding and arrest, or killing if necessary, of Harry Phillips and Jarrod Kilkline could be left safely in his hands.

TWO

January 1866. The New Year.

Moodily Jarrod Kilkline leant against the window, hands in his trousers pockets, staring down at the few squalid buildings outside. Was this year going to be any better than the last? It couldn't be much worse; what with the war ending with the defeat and betrayal of the South and then his enforced flight to Arizona. Followed by all that trouble with Harry Phillips.

No, whatever 1866 held in store it had to be better than 1865. Even if he was stuck here in the middle of absolutely nowhere, making a dubious living as a gambler.

The young girl lying in the bed, which was the tiny room's only decent piece of furniture, stirred and raising herself up on to one elbow, looked over at him.

'What you thinking about, hon?'

Jarrod turned and smiled. 'Nothing, not really.'

Cissie wished that Jarrod would talk to her, tell her what was on his mind. She knew that he was deeply unhappy and wanted to do something to make him feel better.

Jarrod had arrived in town a couple of months ago, looking worn out. At first, Cissie had thought he was just like all the others who came here, stopping a night or two, maybe looking for the odd spot of work so they had enough money to gamble, drink or buy her favours.

Certainly like the others, he was young, no more than twenty-five, with wary eyes, bitter mouth and a gun on his hip he looked ready to use. Tall and thin he had dark hair straggling untidily to his shoulders and wore an ill-fitting assortment of clothes.

Then he'd asked for work, and not just of the casual kind either. He wanted to stay, for a while at least.

The saloon owner, who was Cissie's uncle, had given him a job playing cards, and before long Jarrod had taken up with Cissie.

Cissie was only seventeen but she'd been a prostitute long enough to know practically all there was about men.

She quickly came to realize Jarrod didn't love her but that he was lonely and needed someone to be with and to cling to. And as he was oh so different to her usual customers, being nice and gentle, she was willing to give herself to him for as long as he needed her. For she also realized that he didn't belong here and would leave her soon.

Used to entertaining men on the run, she'd gradually decided Jarrod didn't really fit that role, but because he rarely spoke about himself she couldn't figure out what he was doing at the saloon.

She knew he was still angry over the South's surrender, but she also felt sure he had some deeper secret in his recent past; a secret that gave him nightmares and made him leave his saddlebags under the bed, packed with his few belongings, so he was ready to flee.

'Guess I'd better get up and you'd better go downstairs too. The men'll start coming in soon.'

'Yeah, OK, I will.' Jarrod returned to his gloomy contemplation of the view.

Not there was much to see. The place didn't even have a name. Besides the saloon where he ate, slept and worked, there was only a trader's store and its large corral, a tiny brothel, a livery and some shacks and tents. The streets in between were thick with mud and it was cold. While Jarrod had never gotten used to the overpowering heat of the late summer in Arizona, he now wished for it back. The cold and damp seeped into the wound he'd received in the war and made it ache, his limp becoming more pronounced than usual.

Perhaps he should think about going down near the border, it was always hot there, or so he'd been told. But he'd also been told that the Apaches were making some of their spasmodic trouble along the Gila. Coming from Georgia, he didn't know much about wild Indians, except that he was scared of them.

He'd only asked for a job here because he was used to saloon work, having been a swamper over in Griffin Creek, and now he wondered why he stayed. It wasn't for the pay. It wasn't for Cissie, much as he liked her and sharing her bed. It was mostly because the place had no law.

Promising himself he'd move on soon but wondering whether he would dare risk it, Jarrod put on his coat. Going over to Cissie he hugged her close and kissed her.

'I wish we could stay here, together, forever,' she said clinging to him.

'Me too.' Jarrod was lying. He didn't want to spend the rest of his life in a small room over a dirty saloon, cheating at cards and risking a beating, or worse, from those who lost. He wanted to be back home in Georgia, with things like they used to be and his life not the tangled mess it had become.

Which, like most of Jarrod's dreams, was a hopeless wish that could never come true.

Harry Phillips jigged the horses up the slope of the hill, the wagon creaking and groaning behind him. He stuck out a foot against the front panel, supporting himself as the wheels hit a rock and for a moment threatened to turn the wagon over. As far as he was concerned, horses and wagon were destined for the scrapheap; and so was Bill Brooks the trader they belonged to.

How the hell had he got involved with an idiot like Brooks in the first place? At the time, on the run from the enraged citizens of Griffin Creek and with the collapse of his plans, thanks to that

traitor Kilkline – and after all he'd done for him
too! – the offer of employment had seemed like a
lifeline. No one would look for him with someone
like Brooks.

Phillips had been ready to go to Mexico and hide
out there for a while, until all the fuss and bother
died down, although he hadn't much favoured the
plan. Meeting Brooks down on the border where
the old man was buying whiskey, had provided
both an escape route and, more importantly, the
possibility of money and mayhem.

'Here.' From the seat beside him Brooks handed
Phillips a whiskey flask.

Phillips took a hefty swallow and almost
choked. This was the good stuff, not the watered
down rot gut they sold to the Apaches.

'Like it, do you?' Brooks demanded. 'Bit of a
change from what you drank on the old
plantation, I guess. What was that then? Fancy
French champagne served up by blacks in fancy
uniforms?'

'Something like that. I like this fine.'

'Yeah I can tell that. You've taken to it out here
like you was born to it.'

'It's a helluva lot better than having to obey all
those socially acceptable rules back home.'

'Can't see someone like you following rules.'

Phillips grinned. 'I was the despair of my
parents. They didn't understand me at all. But
then I didn't understand them either, so that was
all right.'

Taking another swallow of whiskey, Phillips

reflected that he sure had come a long way from the days of the plantation in Louisiana. Whoever would have thought that he, the son of the local squire, born to riches and power, with slaves to do everything for him, would be out here in the Arizona desert, driving a wagon loaded with illicit whiskey into the heart of hostile Indian territory?

His old, well-ordered life seemed a whole different world away now, and he wasn't sorry to have left it behind.

For Phillips, who had been going nowhere, the war had provided a way out. It was glorious and he hadn't wanted it to end. Still, life out here in Arizona wasn't all that bad; there was still the chance of killing or being killed.

And now all he had to do was persuade Brooks that they should trade guns as well as whiskey to the Apache. Because that way there was a greater chance that some of the despised Yank soldiers would get killed.

That wasn't proving as easy as he'd hoped. Brooks was a wily old frontiersman who knew too much to listen to Phillips' lying charms.

That evening they came to a halt by the shade of some rocks to make camp. While Phillips saw to the horses and gathered whatever he could to make a fire, Brooks sat back, drinking whiskey and chewing tobacco, taking it easy, letting the younger man do all the work. This didn't please Harry and it was with some difficulty that he held in his easily-lost temper. But he could wait.

While they were waiting for their supper to

cook, Brooks said, 'Been thinking over what you said earlier.' He hawked and spat. 'And I don't like the idea, no sir. Trading whiskey to the Injuns is quite risky enough.'

Goddamn idiot, Phillips said to himself. 'You've been doing it for a long time. You ain't thought much of the risks up till now.'

Brooks was beginning to wish he hadn't taken on this young man. At the time it had been a good idea. Brooks was getting older every day. He'd been trading with the Apaches for many years now and the danger and the environment were taking a toll on his health. A couple more seasons, he reckoned, and then he'd give up, go back East, enjoy some of the money he'd managed to save. In the meantime, a young man down on his luck, willing to do all the hard work would be useful.

But before long Phillips had wanted to be more than a hired hand. He'd wanted to be a partner. And a partner with ideas, who it was difficult to make take 'no' for an answer.

'Trading guns is different. We'd have the army down on us sure enough.'

'Think of the money we'd make. You could retire even earlier than you planned.'

'Money wouldn't be much help iffen I was in the Fort Sherman guardhouse or hanging upside down over an Injun's fire, boiling my brains out because the Apache got greedy.'

'That's a chance you take now surely. And I know where we can get the guns and get 'em cheap.'

'No!' Brooks bashed his hand down on his knees. 'No. It's too dangerous. I don't care about the money. And I ain't too sure it's the money you're most interested in either. You want the danger don't you? Well you can find it some place else. Don't use me for your goddamned games. I'm too old for 'em. I may not have all that many scruples and I've done a few shameful things in my life, but I ain't never started a goddamned Indian war!'

'Keep your britches on old man. You're in charge here.'

'Yeah and don't you forget it. I ain't got to my age by being stupid.'

Phillips' eyes glittered. Well you sure are being stupid now, he thought.

Bill Brooks' come-uppance was about to arrive.

THREE

At first, Jarrod had wondered where all the men in the saloon came from. Friday and Saturday nights were usually crowded and most other nights were reasonably busy too.

Some looked like cowboys, willing to make the long journey from outlying ranches for the sake of company and something to lighten up the monotony of their hard-working lives. A few were farmers or sheepherders; they came in during the week and stayed away at weekends when they were likely to be the butts of the cowboys' jeers and sometimes not very good-natured high jinks.

But most were outlaws on the lam.

Jarrod recognised them all right; vigilant men, with eyes that were never still, who sat with their backs to walls and wore well-cared for guns. He recognized them because he was one of them.

Few of the customers spoke to him, except to curse him. He was a saloon employee and paid to cheat them out of their hard-earned money. No one wanted to be his friend.

Although Tuesday nights were usually amongst

the slowest, when he went downstairs the saloon was already noisy with shouts, laughter and the clink of glasses. Low lamps hung from the ceiling, giving out a foggy glow, sawdust, which was seldomly swept out, covered the floor. The bar was merely some planks laid on barrels, and the only drinks served were poor whiskey and warm beer.

Besides Cissie and himself, the saloon employed two other women, a couple of bartenders and a thug with a shotgun.

In taking on Jarrod, the saloon owner's orders were quite clear: rook the customers for all he could. Jarrod wasn't a particularly good gambler but he'd soon learnt how to be an excellent cheat. What he often wondered was, whose side the thug with the shotgun would be on if he ever got called out. The fact that the last gambler had been lynched by dissatisfied customers didn't bode well for Jarrod's future.

A few farming types had huddled up against the bar, making their glasses of beer last as decently long as they could, and a man who looked like a real hardass desperado was chatting up a whore. Jarrod sat down at his table in the corner, spreading the cards out, playing patience until he was joined by a couple of regulars for a game of desultory poker. As their idea of big spending was to put fifty cents into the pot, he knew he wasn't going to make much that night.

He was just in the middle of a reasonably good hand, courtesy of some dealing off the bottom of the deck, when Cissie came up behind him. A worried look on her face, she bent low and whispered in his ear. 'Jarrod, there's someone over at the livery stable asking about you.'

Jarrod looked at her startled, and scared. His first thought was of Harry Phillips, although on reflection it could be anyone from the law to a bounty hunter. 'What does he look like? Is he tall and dressed in black?'

'No. It's a weedy little man in a check suit and a funny hat. He's got your description and your name. Bert's trying to stall him but he'll soon be here.'

Almost as Cissie stopped speaking, the batwing doors were pushed back.

'Raise you twenty cents,' one of the poker players said.

Jarrod took no notice. He stared at the man who'd just come in. He didn't look like much of a threat; he wasn't wearing a badge or a gun, but he'd asked for Jarrod by name and anyone doing that was unlikely to be friendly. As the man paused to look round, Jarrod threw the cards down on the table.

'I'm out,' he said much to the surprise of the other gamblers. He clutched Cissie round the waist. 'Let's go upstairs.' Quickly, but trying not to attract attention, they went to the stairs at the rear of the saloon.

Once in the room they shared, Jarrod dragged out his saddle-bags from under the bed. He shrugged into his thin outdoors coat and checked his gun, spinning the barrel to make sure it was loaded.

Cissie watched him with wide open eyes. 'Oh, Jarrod, do you have to go?'

'You know I do. Look, if it's not anything, send me word and I'll come back.'

But Cissie noticed that he didn't tell her where he would be. He was leaving, going out of her life, as she had always known he would. Hugging him, crying, she kissed him, knowing she had no choice but to let him go.

As for Jarrod, however much he might regret his hasty departure, what else could he do? Where one man could find him so could others. He shouldn't have stayed this long.

He pulled away. 'Be a good girl,' he said and then as fast as his limp would allow him, he hurried down the back staircase and out into the cold, windy night.

He was just crossing the road towards the livery when the saloon doors opened and a wave of laughter and light spilled out into the street.

'Kilkline! Hey, Jarrod Kilkline!'

It was the weedy looking man!

'Stop!'

Jarrod had no intention of doing that. Instead he put on a spurt of speed, wincing as his leg hurt.

The stableman had been bribed always to have Jarrod's horse ready if anyone came around asking questions. Thank Christ, the man hadn't let him down. The gelding stood in the middle of the runway, saddled and bribed. With a cavalryman's instincts, Jarrod shoved his rifle into its scabbard, swung up into the saddle and urged the horse into the open.

The weedy gent was waiting for him. As he saw that Jarrod wasn't going to stop, he reached for an inside pocket and suddenly a spit of flame lit up the night. Jarrod felt the tug of a bullet ripping through the sleeve of his coat. The bastard had a hide-out gun!

There was no time to do anything except dig heels into the horse's sides. The animal jumped forward with a squeal and banged into Jarrod's pursuer, knocking him off his feet. The man landed on his back in a pile of dirty straw but that didn't stop him getting off a couple more shots, both of which came too close. Whoever the man was, he was a helluva good shot, and not slow to use his gun.

Jarrod dragged his revolver from its holster and turning in the saddle sent back several bullets in reply, all of which missed. He saw a vague outline of the weedy man struggling to his feet, aiming and firing again.

Shouts echoed from the saloon as men rushed out to see what was happening. Naturally there was no sign of the thug with the shotgun; he was never around when you needed him.

Then Jarrod was beyond the buildings, darkness surrounding him, as he headed for the desert. After a while, he paused. Was there pursuit? Over the thudding of his heart, he thought he heard the sound of hoofbeats. Frightened, worried over who the man was,

Jarrod kept going into the cold blackness.

He'd hoped that once the stagecoach robberies stopped, the coach company and the law would stop looking for him. Now he realized how foolish that hope was. He was still being hunted.

'Have you no idea of where Kilkline went? Come on, girl, speak up.'

Cissie stared at the weedy looking gent with tears in her eyes. 'I don't know.'

'You were sleeping with him, weren't you? Didn't he ever talk to you about where he was from or where he might be headed?'

'No.'

'Aw leave the girl alone,' the bartender said, and there were other mutters of disapproval.

Lester Peabody knew when he was in danger from the locals who didn't appreciate his methods. Besides, the girl most likely didn't know anything. Kilkline probably didn't know where he was going himself. It didn't matter much anyway. Peabody had tracked him down this far; he wasn't about to lose him now.

It was a few days later when the scout from Fort Sherman found the body of the old whiskey trader in some rocks near the Gila River. Bill Brooks had been shot to death. There was no sign of his wagon.

Rumour had it that Brooks had recently taken on a partner, a younger man with ruthless blue eyes. For a while the scout searched for a second body. He didn't find it.

He was worried. Rumour had also stated that this young man wanted not only to trade whiskey but guns as well. Brooks might have been a greedy schemer but he hadn't been evil. He'd known quite well that to put guns in the hands of drunken Indians was to ask for trouble no sane man wanted.

The way the scout read it, Brooks' partner had gunned down the old man, and taken considerable pleasure in it too, and stolen the wagon. Even if this particular wagon load only contained whiskey it wouldn't take long for a shrewd businessman to make enough money to fill the next wagon with contraband guns.

Grimly, the scout decided it was time to head back for the Fort to tell Captain Lambert. Let him deal with it.

FOUR

'Sir, do you think there'll be trouble?'

Captain Lambert nodded. 'I'm certain there will be, Sergeant. Bill Brooks was a damned nuisance but at least he only sold whiskey and usually we knew where and when he was likely to sell it. Now … who knows? The Indians are already stirred up because now that the war has ended, more people are coming into what they see as their territory. Getting their hands on guns certainly won't help the situation.'

'It's those goddamned rebels doing this ain't it?' Sergeant McPhee always regretted not getting his hamfisted hands on the group of young men he termed as traitors to the Union.

'We don't know that, Sergeant, but nevertheless I'm inclined to agree with you. The description of the man seen with Brooks sounds very like the leader of the Rebel gang.'

Lambert stood up and went over to the window. He stared out at the dusty parade ground, the flag hanging limp from the flagpole in the windless noonday air. He had few soldiers and a large area to patrol, in which were located a number of hostiles, all quite ready to go on the war path if the circumstances were right. Unless he could do something about that damned renegade trader he, with his whiskey and guns, might just supply the necessary blue touch paper in order to light the fire.

'And as if all that isn't enough,' – Lambert tapped the piece of paper that the messenger had brought to Fort Sherman that morning – 'there's now this.'

The payroll was due to arrive the next day in Griffin Creek under guard, and with the paymaster was Captain Dunlop's daughter, returning from the East where she had been training as a nurse.

'Before I can do anything else, I've first got to ensure the safe arrival of both money and girl at the fort. I've asked Lieutenant Griffiths to head up the patrol that goes to meet them.' He ignored McPhee's groan. 'I want you to go with him.'

'Yes sir.' It wasn't up to McPhee to criticize the decisions of his superior officer but his attitude clearly said that he did not think Lieutenant Griffiths the best person to lead a patrol through possibly dangerous country. He still blamed Lieutenant Griffiths for the failed attempt to arrest the gang of ex-Rebels.

Lambert had no choice. Apart from Captain Dunlop, who was also the post surgeon, and the first lieutenant in charge of the scouts, young Lieutenant Griffiths was his only commissioned officer.

Lieutenant Evan Griffiths, twenty-one, eager, inexperienced and only recently out of West Point, had no such doubts about his abilities. He was proud and pleased. At last Captain Lambert was beginning to realize what a good soldier, a good leader of men, he would make, given the chance.

Having received his orders, he'd almost jumped for joy when he'd left the office. As such behaviour wasn't seemly for an officer, he'd managed to curb his delight. Now he was running backwards and forwards, getting in everyone's way, giving conflicting orders, dancing around in impatience. Not that anyone took much notice of him. The troopers were all more experienced than he was and knew exactly what needed to be done. Besides they knew, even if Evan didn't, that it was Sergeant McPhee who was in charge of this patrol, not the lieutenant.

'Sir, we're almost ready,' McPhee said giving what passed for a salute. 'We can leave in about twenty minutes.'

'That's fine by me, Sergeant.'

'And are you ready, sir?'

'Yes ... er ... well.' Evan blushed furiously, a childish habit that he couldn't seem to grow out of. He had been so busy telling everyone else what to do, he'd forgotten all about himself. Hoping in vain that the sergeant hadn't noticed, he hurried back to Officers Row and the set of rooms he'd been allocated there.

When he'd first arrived at Fort Sherman, Evan had been disappointed. It wasn't a bit like he'd imagined. There was no stockade, no look-out towers, no orderly set of work buildings.

Instead the place looked more like a village than a fort: merely a motley collection of untidy buildings grouped haphazardly round a parade ground in the middle of a flat, colourless meadow. One line of the square was taken up by the post headquarters, and opposite that Officers Row. Another side consisted of the post trader's store and the enlisted men's bunkhouses, while the fourth was a jumble of stables, blacksmith's, large corral and the guardhouse.

There was always plenty going on. Soldiers hurried backwards and forwards, doing whatever it was they had to do; a number of civilians came to the Fort on business; emigrants halted to replenish their supplies at the sutler's store.

Evan had quickly discovered that the fort was seriously undermanned and he was almost Captain Lambert's only serving officer. Thus the rooms he'd been given were really meant for someone of much higher rank than himself and he had bedroom, kitchen and a sitting-room. With the help of Mrs Lambert and the wife of the first lieutenant he'd managed to make the rooms quite comfortable and placed round them various photographs of the members of his family.

The photographs made him feel better for he was very lonely, missing his folks and someone of his own age to talk to. There were plenty of young men amongst the troopers but naturally he couldn't converse with them. He'd also been well aware of what they thought of him and the harder he'd tried the worse their mockery became. His first letters home had been bravely written but couldn't disguise his homesickness.

So this patrol was very important to him. It wasn't the first patrol he'd led and in his heart he felt it wasn't much of an assignment, unlikely to involve any danger – no wild charges against marauding whooping Apaches, no deeds of heroic bravery. But if all went well then hopefully Captain Lambert would trust him with more and more.

Evan had another reason for wanting to do well: Hazel Dunlop.

He'd seen her photograph in the surgeon's house. She looked very pretty and he couldn't wait to meet her and make a good impression. Quite how he was going to do that, Evan didn't know. Girlfriends weren't allowed at West Point and before going there he had been much too shy to squire around any of the local girls. He'd danced with a few at parties given by family and friends, kissed one of the family maids who'd slapped him round the face for it, and written love letters to the girl down the street, which he'd never dared post; and that was his sum knowledge of females. However, he was now twenty-one, an army officer and thus a man and quite different to the shy boy. Or at least that was what he hoped.

As Evan was buckling on his sabre, Captain Dunlop knocked on the door and came in.

'Ah, you're off then?'

'Yes, sir.'

'Good. You know, Lieutenant, my daughter is

very precious to me. I'm trusting you to look after her.'

'I will, sir,' Evan replied seriously; 'you can rely on me.'

Doctor Dunlop hid a smile. Poor Lieutenant Griffiths, so earnest, so well meaning, so desperate to succeed. It was unlikely that he'd long remain the same, not stuck out here at Fort Sherman.

When Jarrod decided he was safe he came to a halt amongst some hills overlooking a small waterhole. Anxiously he scanned his back trail, as he had done on several occasions. No one was pursuing him, at least not at the moment.

He had travelled fast for several days, resting only when he had to, changing his route, trying to keep to the rocks and streams where hopefully his tracks would be hard to follow. The land he crossed was empty and desolate, nothing but scrub grass, sandy soil and sagebrush.

Where should he go?

Taking his bearings, he realized, with a shock, that he was quite near Griffin Creek. Well, he couldn't go there and he couldn't go south because that was where the Apaches were. Behind him somewhere was the weedy gent. That left north – Utah or Colorado.

But first he'd make camp here and rest up awhile. He was oh so tired and so was his horse. It was a good spot with water and game. He'd surely be safe for a couple of days.

* * *

On the outskirts of Griffin Creek, Lieutenant Griffiths had taken charge of the paymaster's wagon and now he and the troopers waited outside the hotel for Miss Hazel Dunlop. The girl was inside freshening up from the long journey she had just undertaken, before starting on the final leg to Fort Sherman.

At last, the door opened and the girl emerged. Evan gaped. She was so much prettier than her photograph.

She was about nineteen and being hatless he could see she had long brown hair that curled to her shoulders. She also had brown eyes, a full mouth and a pale complexion. And a most wonderful figure, shown off delightfully in the divided skirt and shirt she was wearing.

She was also staring at him and Evan had no idea of what to do.

'Lieutenant,' McPhee prompted from behind him.

'M … Miss Hazel Dunlop,' Evan managed to say in a strangled stutter.

'That's right. And you are?'

'Lieutenant Evan Griffiths. I'm here to escort you to Fort Sherman.' He saluted smartly and ignoring, but very aware of, the sniggers from the troopers, he jumped off his horse and hovered round the girl. He was very red and nervous, cursing himself for being so awkward, knowing he was hardly making the masterful impression he'd dreamt of. 'Are you ready?'

'Yes, thank you.'

'Would you like to ride in the wagon or would you prefer to ride a horse?'

'I'd like to ride if I can. That wagon is awfully bumpy and hot. But I don't want to put anyone to any trouble.'

'You won't. Sergeant McPhee, arrange that will you?' Evan gave the order in his most haughty manner, determined to let everyone, especially Miss Dunlop, know that he was in charge.

'Yes, sir, at once sir. Trooper Donnolly you ride in the wagon and let Miss Dunlop have your horse.'

Because Evan was too busy fussing with Hazel to remember to do so, McPhee gave orders placing the troopers in formation around the wagon. Before long, they set out from Griffin Creek, spurs jingling, leather creaking, the Company flag fluttering in the breeze, on the way back to Fort Sherman.

Evan and Hazel rode out in front. Evan longed to make sparkling conversation but couldn't think of a thing to say. Luckily the girl seemed quite happy to ride along in silence staring at the scenery.

About midday, McPhee rode forward. 'Lieutenant, there's a waterhole up ahead. Wouldn't it be a good idea to stop, rest the horses and the men?'

Evan turned towards him. 'Of course it would, Sergeant. I was just about to suggest it.' He was cross, embarrassed because he had had no such idea in mind. 'We'll rest for an hour ...'

'Two hours might be better, sir, seeing as how the horses are tired.'

'Two hours then.' Evan smiled nervously at Hazel hoping she didn't think him a fool. Wisely she pretended not to have heard this exchange.

There were times when Evan felt he really would have to speak to McPhee about the way he acted but with the man being so much bigger than him, maybe that time hadn't yet come.

Surrounded by rocks and trees, the waterhole made an oasis of blue and green in the desert grey. Encroaching hills, covered with ponderosa pine and cedar, provided welcome shade and a cooling breeze.

There was sign of animals making their way to the water to drink but not of any other human being.

Even so McPhee took no chances. He ordered several of the troopers to climb into the hills and make sure no Indians lurked there.

Evan had nothing like duty or danger on his mind. All he could think of was Miss Dunlop and the fact they had been riding together all morning. Now he led her a little way from the rest of the men and, as their horses dipped their heads towards the water, said, 'Would you care to accompany me on a short walk?' He wished he didn't sound so formal but he couldn't help himself.

'Is it safe?'

'We won't go far. Besides I'll be there to protect you.'

Hazel smiled at him. 'Yes, let's then. I could do with stretching my legs.'

Evan blushed at her use of the word 'legs'; at home his mother always referred to them as 'limbs', if she allowed reference to them at all.

Leaving the horses they wandered off along by the waterhole and were soon lost to sight.

Gradually the place settled down. The animals were cared for, the men drank their fill and, as there wasn't time to light a fire, ate some cold rations, then lay down on the ground to rest.

McPhee stood alone by the water. He didn't like the lieutenant and the girl going off like that. There probably wasn't any danger but he felt responsible for them both. They could hardly be expected to look after themselves and Captain Lambert was depending on him. All the same he didn't see how he could have stopped them. The lieutenant wouldn't appreciate any more interference, especially when he so badly wanted to prove to the girl how capable he was and that he, not his sergeant, was the one in command.

What it was to be young and foolish! McPhee couldn't remember being either.

The sergeant's troubled thoughts were disturbed by shouts from halfway up the hill behind him. He flung round. Now what? Puzzled, ready for trouble, the troopers started to get to their feet.

'What's up?' Corporal Hall called. 'Apaches?'

'No! Look!' Someone else pointed up the hill.

Two of the soldiers McPhee had sent up there

came into view. Between them, they were holding a struggling young man, dragging him down the slope. Sensing excitement, the troopers all crowded forward.

As they got to the waterhole, the prisoner yelled, 'Let me go, you bastards!'

Eyes gleaming, McPhee walked up to the three men.

'He was up there watching us,' Trooper Donnolly explained. 'When we challenged him he made a run for it.'

'I haven't done anything! Let me go!'

McPhee stood, hands on hips, staring at the young man in front of him. The Georgian accent was unmistakable. This was one of the Rebels who'd made such a lot of trouble for everyone last year.

McPhee grinned.

FIVE

'How long before we reach the fort?' Hazel asked as she and Evan came to a halt by some low rocks. She sat on one and he stood protectively beside her, hand resting on the top of his sabre. Before them a valley spread out to the far horizon of the mauvey-blue mountains, the air sweet with the smell of sagebrush.

'Tomorrow evening, if the weather holds good. Will you mind camping out?'

Hazel laughed, shaking her head. 'I'm used to it after the last few days. I slept in the wagon. I must say I didn't like the idea at first but everyone was so nice and polite. You forget, Lieutenant Griffiths, that I'm a soldier's daughter.'

'Your father is looking forward to seeing you again.'

'I want to see him as well. I haven't done so for a couple of years now, since I went back East to start my studies.'

'You're studying to be a nurse, aren't you?'

'That's right. I've always wanted to be a nurse, right from when I was a little girl. When I was old enough to start training Papa and I were in Texas, and it was decided that I would be better off going to live with my aunt and uncle and attending school in Michigan.'

'And do you like nursing?'

'Oh yes, I love it! It's all I ever thought it would be. But I missed Papa very much and the wide open spaces. Towns are all right, they can be exciting, but they're awfully crowded and there's so little freedom. For instance, I'd never be allowed to be out here with you all by myself, there would have to be a chaperone in the background.'

Hazel laughed at such foolishness but Evan went red. He hardly dared think of what his mother would say if she could see him now, in such close proximity to a young, unmarried female with no one else in sight. Or what she would think of Hazel's morals, in allowing such a thing. Yet there could hardly be anything more innocent than their stroll together.

Never having been tongue-tied herself, Hazel realized that the poor lieutenant was painfully shy and that it was an effort for him to make conversation with her. Now, in an attempt to get him to talk about himself, she said, 'And, Lieutenant, what about you? Do you like it out here? Do you like Fort Sherman?'

Evan didn't feel he could admit how much he hadn't liked it at first. That would sound self-pitying. So he said, 'It's very different to what I was used to. I come from the East, near New

York. Nothing that I learned at West Point prepared me for reality. For instance, most of the men don't wear the regulation uniform, they add bits and pieces to it as they please and some of them don't even carry sabres, even though the regulations state they should.'

Evan's uniform was as clean and tidy as he could make it, boots shone every day, trousers with a pressed pleat down the front, shirt buttons done up. He himself always had a neat, short haircut and he shaved every day. Of course, now, he, like everyone else, was covered in a layer of dust but at least he wasn't wearing anything but the correct hat and gauntlets, and carrying the weaponry laid down in the army manuals.

'Oh dear! Does it matter?'

'A sloppy soldier, Miss Dunlop, is a sloppy fighter.'

Hazel looked suitably chastened.

'Captain Lambert is a good man though. All the men look up to him. He'd do anything for them and they know it. He's a good officer too. He knows only too well the dangers of the boredom of a frontier fort and has ordered that the men be kept busy with drills. They march, ride and practise with weapons for at least part of the day, and that can only be good for them and their morale. Sergeant McPhee has also started a post baseball team.'

As a lieutenant, Evan sometimes led the man in their drill but didn't feel able to join in with their leisure activities; something that had marked him out not as shy, which he was, but unapproachable, which he didn't want to be.

'I can't understand why the captain has been passed over for promotion.'

'There are many men like that in the army. It's the flamboyant ones who get noticed. Does he mind?'

'I don't know.' Captain Lambert didn't exactly confide his feelings to his young lieutenant. 'I think he likes it out here.'

'Most people do when they get to know the desert. You will too, Evan, I'm sure.'

He went red again and got all embarrassed at her use of his given name. She was practically the first girl who'd ever called him by it, for in the society where he came from couples had practically to be married before they could start to use each other's Christian names. While he hadn't given it much thought before, he now decided he was beginning to like the West where such informality hardly mattered. Still it would be a long time before he could call Miss Dunlop, Hazel; the very thought made him nervous.

The quiet, pleasant interlude was suddenly broken by the sound of running feet crashing through the undergrowth. As Evan swung round drawing his sabre, and Hazel sprang to her feet behind him, Corporal Hall burst into view.

'Lieutenant! Lieutenant!' he gasped. 'You'd better come quick!'

Jarrod was not only angry at being dragged down to the waterhole, he was also scared. And with good reason.

Here he was, all alone, an ex-Rebel, surrounded by Union soldiers, who, only a short while ago, he'd been at war with. He hated the North and what the North was doing to the South and he had no reason to believe that these men would treat him kindly.

Even worse was the sergeant. Jarrod recognized him from last year. He was the one who'd chased him to Griffin Creek. It was impossible to forget him. In his early forties, the man was over six feet tall with a well-muscled chest and thick arms. He was already flexing his hands into fists, for it seemed the sergeant had also recognized him.

McPhee reached out, taking hold of a handful of Jarrod's hair, jerking his head back. 'You're one of them bastards we had the trouble with last year ain't you? And now you've taken up whiskey trading with the Apache.'

'I don't know what the hell you're talking about,' Jarrod protested, trying unsuccessfully to pull away from the sergeant's grasp.

'Guns too or so we've heard.'

'Goddamned trouble-maker,' someone else muttered.

McPhee nodded to the soldiers holding Jarrod. 'Take his gun away from him,' he said. Then as they let Jarrod go, McPhee flung him halfway across the small encampment. 'Take your coat off,' he ordered, beginning to unbutton his own jacket.

'Why? What for?' Jarrod knew exactly why.

'Because asshole I'm going to give you exactly what you deserve, you goddamned filthy traitor!'

Jarrod backed away from the man. There was no way he could stand up to the huge sergeant. He was going to get beaten up for sure; how badly depended on his opponent. And none of the others was about to help him. They'd already formed up in a circle, faces alight with savage pleasure. It just confirmed all that Jarrod had ever thought about Yankee bluebellies.

'You bastard!' he yelled and, bending down grabbed a handful of sand, flinging it at the sergeant's face, rushing towards him.

Taken by surprise, McPhee stumbled and Jarrod got in one smashing blow on the man's jaw, rocking him back on his heels.

McPhee recovered swiftly and lunged out, hitting Jarrod so hard he reeled from the force of it. The sergeant then grabbed him round the waist, hitting him hard in the ribs. Jarrod broke away and kicked out at the man, hoping to bring his knee up into the sergeant's groin. Yelling, McPhee twisted so that Jarrod's knee found only his thigh. The respite was short and soon McPhee was coming on again.

Aware of yells of encouragement and excitement, the circle of faces spinning all round him, Jarrod was knocked to the ground. McPhee's boot connected with his wounded leg and tears of pain blurred his vision. Then he was being dragged up again and a blow to his head caused stars to explode in his brain.

Somehow, Jarrod kept struggling to his feet, determined to show them all what Southerners were made of, even though his leg would hardly support him and he couldn't even hobble out of the way of the sergeant's fists. Swaying, blood blinding his eyes, getting in his mouth, he had no way of stopping McPhee hitting him.

The next time he fell, he had no strength or willpower left to do anything but lay there and take it.

Through ringing ears, Jarrod thought he heard someone say, 'Hey come on, Sarge, leave him alone he's had enough,' before a foot lashed against the back of his head. He felt himself go limp, as if he was a ragdoll that had suddenly lost all its stuffing. It seemed as if he was falling again, even though he was already on the ground, and then everything went black and he felt nothing more.

As Evan and Corporal Hall rushed back to the waterhole, McPhee was still kicking the now unconscious Jarrod. The excitement of the troopers around him had long since turned to disgust, but they were all too frightened of the sergeant to stop him.

Evan was also frightened of the man, who looked quite mad, but his own horror and anger was echoed by Hazel's cry of 'Oh no!' and he knew he had to do something.

'Sergeant McPhee!' he yelled. 'Stop that!' And he ran up to the man, plunging between him and the inert body on the ground.

McPhee's eyes blazed with fury and for a moment it seemed as if he was going to turn on his lieutenant. Then a couple of the troopers dashed forward, catching hold of his arms, pulling him out of the way.

'My God, McPhee, I'll have you up on a charge for this!'

'He's a Rebel, a trouble-maker,' McPhee had his head down, panting.

'I don't care who he is! And you men, how could you let it happen?' Evan glared round at the troopers, who stared at him with hangdog expressions or refused to look at him at all. But how could he be angry with them when he'd walked away, thinking only of himself and Hazel Dunlop, and left McPhee to do as he pleased? The fact that no one could have foreseen this was no excuse. He'd deserted his post.

'Get him out of my sight,' he ordered Corporal Hall and then turned to where Hazel was gently stroking the long hair out of the eyes of the unconscious man. 'Oh God.'

The young man's face was a mess of cuts, blood and bruises. There was a deep gash across his cheek, both eyes were bruised, lips swollen and torn. When Hazel undid his shirt it was to reveal signs of bruises already purpling along his ribs and back.

'I can't do anything for him, except bathe his wounds with water. I've nothing with me.' There were tears in the girl's eyes. 'Oh, Evan, how could he have done it?' This was the other side of the frontier, the one she didn't, could never, like.

'McPhee is a law unto himself. He thought he had a reason.'

'There could be no reason for continuing to kick someone who was plainly unconscious!'

'I know,' Evan agreed unhappily. He nodded at the corporal. 'Get a couple of men to carry him to the wagon. And send someone to fetch his horse and anything else he had with him. Miss Dunlop, will you make him as comfortable as you can?'

So Jarrod was laid in the wagon and covered with a blanket. He groaned once or twice but otherwise made no sound and he didn't move.

Evan feared that if they didn't reach the fort soon, he might die.

SIX

Jarrod groaned in his sleep, moved restlessly and blinked open his eyes.

'Don't move,' a woman's voice said and a cool hand placed itself on his forehead.

It was dark, or at least he thought it was dark because he could hardly see, everything was a blur. His head ached, his eyes ached, in fact, come to think of it his whole body ached. His leg hurt so much he felt sick. He realized he was lying on his back and beneath the rough blanket that covered him, he was naked.

'How do you feel?' the disembodied voice asked.

'I …' Jarrod faltered to a halt. It was as if his lips wouldn't work. He swallowed and began again. 'I hurt all over.'

'Just lie still. Here.' A glass was placed against his mouth. 'Careful, just a sip. Now try to go back to sleep.'

Jarrod closed his eyes and drifted back into unconsciousness again. It seemed later that all this happened several times and that each time the woman was there to help him. But he wasn't

sure, maybe it was part of an uncomfortable
dream.

Then at last when he woke, he could see
properly. And he wasn't reassured.

The small room was bare, its only furniture the
narrow bed on which he lay, and a chair on which
stood a glass of water. There was a heavy oak door
with a grille in it, floor and walls of adobe and a
tiny barred window.

He was in prison!

Scared, Jarrod tried to sit up but groaning sank
back again. What had happened? Where was he?
Reaching up a shaky hand he touched his lips.
They were swollen and there was a nasty bump
over one eye, while his ribs felt like they were
broken.

Christ! The bluecoat soldiers at the waterhole!
The sergeant! Oh Christ, where *was* he?

The door to the cell opened and a young woman
came in. She smiled. 'Ah awake at last!' She
crossed over to the bed, touching his face and
forehead with a competent hand. 'And the fever
has gone. You're well on the way to recovery. Do
you want some water?'

'Yes please,' Jarrod replied in a dry, croaky
voice.

She lifted the glass to his lips. 'Take it easy,
don't try to move. I'll go and get you some soup.'

'I'm not hungry.'

'You must eat to get your strength back. Try a
few mouthfuls. For me.'

'Who are you?'

'My name's Hazel Dunlop. I'm the surgeon's daughter and I'm also a nurse.'

'Where am I?'

'Fort Sherman.'

And she went out leaving Jarrod alone with all his worst fears confirmed.

'Of course I'm not a real nurse, not yet,' Hazel confessed, when she returned and sat on the narrow bed and carefully spoonfed Jarrod. 'I'm in the middle of my training.'

After a few mouthfuls he shook his head and unlike the medics in the army hospital where he'd ended up in the Civil War she didn't force him to eat what he didn't want.

'Luckily nothing was broken. Which is a wonder considering the beating that bully of a sergeant gave you! I feared that at the very least some of your ribs were broken or that maybe you'd lose the use of your eye.' Hazel's own eyes darkened in remembrance at the ugly scene. 'What I find so hard to forgive is that McPhee continued to kick you when you were on the ground. He must have known you were unable to defend yourself or even move out of his way.'

'Sometimes blood-lust takes over good sense.'

'That's no excuse. Anyway Evan, that's Lieutenant Griffiths, intervened and almost got hurt himself. He got you back here as quickly as he could. We only slept a couple of hours that night. And then Papa treated you.'

'You've been the one here with me all the time haven't you?'

'You know how it is. The doctor sees the patient, pronounces that he needs care and attention and the nurse is left to do all the work.'

Jarrod grinned, then wished he hadn't as his cut and swollen lips hurt.

'I'm only glad I was here to help. Mrs Lambert, she's the commanding officer's wife, has sat with you as well, but she's so busy with her duties round the fort she obviously couldn't do so for long.'

'How long have I been here?'

'Ten days. Now get some sleep, that's the best thing for you right now.'

Jarrod put out a hand to stop her leaving. 'Miss Hazel, this is the guardhouse isn't it, not the hospital? Am I under arrest?'

Hazel looked at him in surprise. 'Why, I don't know ... You haven't done anything have you? Except be the victim of an assault and that's not a crime.'

'I'm a Southerner.'

'What's that got to do with anything? The Civil War is over.'

A little later Captain Dunlop came in to see his patient. He poked here and there, ignoring Jarrod's moans.

'On behalf of Captain Lambert I want to apologize for what McPhee did. It was inexcusable. He's been busted back to private for it. And not before time.'

Jarrod shivered. 'Supposing he takes that out on me?'

'He won't. He's had his fun and now it's

finished. Besides it won't be long before Captain Lambert promotes him back to sergeant. Unfortunately, McPhee is a good soldier and we all depend on him. I see you have an old wound in your leg. Get it in the war?'

'Yes, sir.'

'Hurt much?'

'Sometimes. It's something I've got to live with. I feared they might amputate it. And a lot more got hurt worse. Am I OK?'

Dunlop nodded. 'All the bruises and swellings are going down nicely. You were an extremely lucky young man.'

'So your daughter said,' Jarrod found he couldn't exactly feel the same way. He'd been beaten up, he was a prisoner at Fort Sherman where they knew all about the stagecoach robberies and it seemed quite likely that, despite what the surgeon said, Sergeant McPhee might well blame him for his demotion. At best he'd be hauled off to Griffin Creek and jail, at worst they'd decide to hang him right here at the fort. He was a Southern Rebel amongst Yankee soldiers. There didn't seem to be much luck involved in that!

His luck didn't improve over much when Captain Lambert came to see him.

Sitting down on the end of the bed, Lambert looked at him and said, 'So you're Jarrod Kilkline?'

And Jarrod felt too hurt and tired to even try to deny the fact. He nodded. 'Yeah, that's right.'

'Well, son, you've sure made a mess of things

haven't you? What am I going to do with you? You know there's a warrant out for your arrest for robbery and murder.'

'Murder?' Jarrod looked at the man with shocked eyes. 'I haven't murdered anyone.'

'The stagecoach guard that was killed, remember?'

'I didn't kill him. Harry Phillips did that.'

'You were there.'

'Oh God.' Jarrod sighed with despair. He was ashamed to feel tears squeezing out of the sides of his eyes but could do nothing to stop them.

'What made you take up with the likes of Phillips in the first place? From all I've heard you don't seem the type.'

'I was bitter, and lonely. He and the others were Southerners like me. And Harry can be charming and plausible when he wants to. What's more, at first I didn't believe what we were doing was wrong. I wanted to start up a new Southern army. When I realized how crazy the idea was, I quit the gang.'

'Well, it's not me you've got to convince, it's a judge and jury. Perhaps the citizens of Griffin Creek will be willing to listen to your story. Perhaps they won't. But you must see that I've got to turn you over to them. And you've got to be man enough to face up to what you did.' But Lambert didn't speak unkindly.

'Have you sent for the law yet?'

'No. I decided you weren't in any fit state to travel anywhere at the moment. You get well first, then you can be taken back to Griffin Creek. By the way, son,' Lambert's voice hardened, 'have you ever been involved with a whiskey trader named Brooks?'

'The sergeant said something about that. And about guns as well. No, I haven't. Why do you think I might have been?'

'We believe that one of you Rebels was helping Brooks. And McPhee is right. It's quite probable that that same person is now running guns to the Apache.'

'It must be Harry Phillips then. It would be just like him.'

'Any idea of where he'd get guns from? Look,' Lambert went on as Jarrod paused, 'I can't promise you that if you help me I can make things easier for you but think about the men and women, red and white, who are going to be killed because of your friend.'

'Harry isn't my friend and I don't owe him anything.'

'Well then?'

'A few months back we had dealings with a family down near the Gila. We were cheated and Harry was spitting mad. That wouldn't stop him dealing with them if he thought he could make money or mischief out of it.'

'Do you know the name of this family?'

'It was Barnes.'

'Ah yes, Ezekial Barnes. I know all about him. He and his two sons were killed just the other day, their house burnt to the ground and presumably all their guns stolen. I thought Indians were responsible but from what you've told me it could be this Phillips.'

'Yeah, it could. Revenge and profit all in one fell swoop.'

That evening as Jarrod lay in the bed, he could hear music; a piano was being played and men's voices mingled with that of girlish laughter. Somewhere they were having a party. Perhaps even a dance. He remembered the last dance he'd been to, in Griffin Creek, where for a few short hours he'd enjoyed some happiness. Now he wondered if he would ever go to a dance again. It didn't seem likely.

Instead of being with other people, he lay here all alone, and afraid.

'Mr Kilkline always looks so sad,' Hazel said to Evan, as Evan brought her a glass of lemonade.

'I'm not surprised. I'd look sad if I was going to spend the rest of my life in jail.'

Evan sounded annoyed. Hazel had been so concerned about her patient that he had seen hardly anything of her since getting back to the fort. He wasn't exactly jealous. He felt sure that Hazel's interest in Jarrod Kilkline stemmed from the fact that he was someone she could practise her nursing skills on. But even here, all the girl wanted to do was talk about him. It wasn't fair. Evan almost wished it was he who was hurt or sick so that Hazel could care for him.

Mrs Lambert's party, given in honour of Hazel's

arrival, wasn't a very large one, limited as it was to the officers at the fort and their women. But Mrs Lambert had gone to a lot of trouble to make sure everyone who could attend was available to do so; thus the delay between Hazel reaching the fort and the party, because the first lieutenant had been out with his scouts.

Hard work had gone into making it as happy an occasion as possible. Coloured lanterns hung from the ceiling; there was weak punch, pretty sandwiches and cakes and the wife of the first lieutenant was playing the piano. However small, it was still a welcome break in the monotony of the fort life.

'Captain Dunlop has told me how much of an improvement you've made to his life and to his house since you arrived.' Mrs Lambert came up to them, putting an arm round Hazel's waist. 'Curtains at the windows, flowers in vases, and everything neat and polished.'

Hazel smiled. 'And I'm going to plant vegetables in the garden. If they grow they will make a variety to our diet.'

'We could all do with that.' Elizabeth Lambert was forty, with greying brown hair, pulled into a neat simple bun, and sad brown eyes. With her sharp intuition, there was very little that happened around the post that escaped her. She knew that young Lieutenant Griffiths was in love with Miss Hazel Dunlop, and that Hazel probably wouldn't be too unwilling to receive his advances. Unfortunately, he was unlikely to do anything about it, unless perhaps given a helping hand.

'Hazel, dear, you've certainly been very busy, what with all your nursing duties as well. You can hardly have had any time to yourself.'

'I don't mind, Mrs Lambert.'

'I know but how would it be if, now that Mr Kilkline is getting better, I looked after him tomorrow and Evan accompanied you on a short ride? Just to the stream and back; it's quite nice country and near enough to the fort to be safe. Would you like that?'

'Oh, yes, thank you. That is if Evan, er Lieutenant Griffiths can find the time.' Hazel smiled at Evan, who went very red.

There was no doubt about his reaction to the proposal. His heart leapt with both pleasure and anxiety; he would all be alone with Hazel!

'I'll speak to my husband. Leave it to me.'

Later as she and Captain Lambert stood on the porch watching their guests leave, she put her plan into action. 'They're both so young and will have little time together. If their romance is to flourish, they'll need to get to know one another better before she has to go back East to continue her nursing.'

Lambert smiled. 'I'll see what I can do. But with the scouts returning every day with tales of growing Indian trouble, I'll soon need him to take out a patrol and investigate.'

'He's so young and inexperienced and it could be dangerous.'

'I know but Griffiths is a soldier and must take his chances as we all do.'

Elizabeth sighed and took hold of her husband's hand. 'Is it really as bad as that?'

'Yes. I'm thinking about ordering all the small ranchers round here to come closer to the protection of the fort until things settle down.'

'They won't like that.'

'They'll like losing their scalps even less.'

SEVEN

Mrs Lambert swept into Jarrod's cell. 'Well now, Mr Kilkline, how are you feeling this morning? You look a lot better, I must say. Do you think you can get up today?'

'Yes.' Jarrod was getting bored lying in bed. He knew who Mrs Lambert was, for she had taken turns with Hazel in feeding him. He could eat quite well now, although he still had difficulty chewing.

Mrs Lambert also knew all about Jarrod Kilkline. Her husband always discussed his problems with her. The young man had been a fool but all the same she couldn't help feeling sorry for him; who knew how anyone would behave when it seemed there was nothing left in his life? At the same time she knew her husband had no choice but to hand him over to the law.

'Perhaps you can sit outside for a little while?'

'I don't know about that.'

'Why not? It's a lovely day. It'll be much more pleasant sitting in the open than being cooped up in here.'

'I'll be out there, alone, amongst Yankee soldiers.'

Mrs Lambert laughed. 'They won't eat you.'

'I'm a Southerner, a Rebel, they know I fought in the war.'

'Most of them were out here during the war. It was nothing to do with them. They won't hold a grudge if you won't.'

'What about the Captain? Won't he mind?'

'My dear Mr Kilkline, I hardly think you're fit enough to make a break for it. And you really wouldn't be that stupid, would you, not when there are armed Yankees all over the place just waiting their chance to shoot down a Rebel?'

Reluctantly Jarrod smiled at her. 'All right.'

'Have you finished your breakfast? Good. I'll get Corporal Hall to help you.'

A few minutes later Corporal Hall came in. 'Come on, old son, let's get you up.'

The man put his arms around Jarrod's shoulders and helped him out of bed. He'd brought with him someone's nightshirt and a dressing-robe, which he had to help Jarrod put on because now he'd got up and was on his feet, Jarrod found he was too weak to dress himself.

'You know that Mrs Lambert is a real fine lady, ain't she? You'd never know how much loss she's suffered.'

'What do you mean?'

'Her and the cap'n had one son, Christopher, apple of their eye by all accounts. Got injured in the war and now lives with his grandparents back

in New York. He'll never recover. Got shot at
Chickamauga. Were you there?'

'No. Would it have mattered if I was?'

'Guess not. Soldiers get used to having to shoot
at one another. Ain't nothing personal in it, not
usually anyhow. Right you're ready. Lean on me
and we'll get you outside.'

Although the journey was only a few steps,
Jarrod was glad to sit down, his legs feeling shaky
as if they wouldn't support him. Mrs Lambert put
a blanket over his knees. Then he was left alone.
Despite her reassuring words, and Corporal Hall's
gruff kindness, he felt most uncomfortable here in
the fort amongst so many soldiers in blue. But
they took very little notice of him. One or two
stared at him curiously as if he might have horns
and cloven hoofs, but as soon as they saw he was a
man just the same as them, they lost interest.

His worst moment came when ex-Sergeant
McPhee approached him. The man's jacket clearly
showed where his stripes had once been and his
face showed even more clearly exactly what he felt
about the situation. He came to a halt a few feet
away, glaring.

Scared, Jarrod got to his feet, losing his blanket
and toppling the chair over.

'Goddamned Reb, sitting there like you ain't got
any troubles in the world. When this is all your
fault.' Angrily, McPhee indicated his stripeless
sleeves. 'Thanks to you I'm the laughing stock of
the post.'

This was so unfair that Jarrod, who felt it would

be wisest to keep quiet, had to defend himself. 'It was hardly my fault you beat me senseless.'

'You were a Reb weren't you? Thanks to bastards like you, thousands of good Northern boys got killed.'

'So did Southerners.'

McPhee ignored this. 'And there might be a lot more good soldiers who yet die because of that bastard Reb trading guns with the Apaches.'

'That's nothing to do with me.'

'The captain believes you; I ain't so sure.'

'It's the truth,' Jarrod said a bit desperately.

'Oh don't look so worried, I ain't about to touch you again, got orders see. But I shouldn't get too comfortable. There might come a time when those who give out the orders ain't around.'

Sulkily, Jarrod breathed a sigh of relief as the big man turned on his heel and marched away. Shaking, he picked up the chair and sat down, cursing himself for being so weak and unable to defend himself but right then, there was nothing he could do about it.

'Let's gallop!' Hazel cried, and, putting spurs to her horse, rode away from Evan.

He watched her for an appreciative moment; her hair streaming out behind her, the way she handled her horse, before he raced her to the stream.

'You let me win,' she accused, laughing as they came to a halt.

They had brought a picnic with them and,

dismounting, leading their horses, they walked along side by side, until they came to a spot shaded by cypress and larch, the branches whispering in the breeze, and where the blue water raced over white stones. Evan laid his saddle blanket on the ground so they could sit down.

'Oh it's so lovely here,' Hazel said. 'It seems such a pity that there has to be so much fighting over the land. Why can't people live in peace?'

'I think part of the trouble is that we're so different to the Indians. We like staying put, making a home for ourselves and setting down roots for our families in the future. We also like towns and material goods. The Indians aren't like that. They're nomads and they don't care much for improving themselves because they're happy as they are. Who can say who is right or wrong?'

'They also like fighting and killing.'

'Wouldn't you fight if you saw strangers coming in and taking your home from you?'

'They're cruel and merciless.'

'Some pretty cruel and merciless things have been done to them too.'

'If you feel that way then why are you a soldier?'

'I don't believe they're necessarily right, merely that there are two sides to every question. Please, don't let's argue.'

'I'm not arguing. I like listening to other people's opinions.' Hazel smiled. She leant back, resting on her elbows. 'I wish I could stay here forever.'

'You are going back then?' Evan's voice couldn't hide his disappointment.

Hazel turned to him. 'I must. I have my training to finish.'

'When are you going?'

'Oh not for a month or more.'

Good, Evan thought, time enough surely for him to pluck up the courage necessary to tell her how he felt, or at least ask her permission to write to her. He longed to take her in his arms and kiss her, but how could he when he didn't know what to do? So far he hadn't even tried to hold her hand.

Extremely properly, they sat together for the rest of the afternoon, hardly speaking, not touching, until it was time to go back to the fort.

Back in his cell, Jarrod stood at the window, watching as the young lieutenant and Hazel came back from their ride. They'd been out riding every afternoon for the last week. Hazel then always came to see how her patient was doing. Allowing, as usual, her tongue to run away with her, she'd told Jarrod how much she liked Evan but how exasperated she was becoming with his inability to do more than worship her from afar. Hazel was a modern young lady and didn't appreciate being put on a pedestal.

'Why don't you tell him how you feel?'

'Oh no, I couldn't.' Hazel wasn't that modern. 'Anyway it would only frighten him all the more. Sometimes men are so silly.'

'He can't help being shy.'

'I know. But surely he knows me well enough by now to at least tell me he loves me even if he hasn't got the courage to show me.' Frustration was making Hazel bad tempered. 'He won't even call me Hazel, even though I've asked him to, but persists in saying "Miss Dunlop".'

Jarrod looked forward to Hazel's visits. Apart from fleeting glimpses in on him by Mrs Lambert. she was the only one who came and actually talked to him. And now that he was getting better and could eat, dress and walk all by himself, Captain Lambert had ordered that he should no longer be allowed to sit outside.

So Jarrod's world was confined to his small dark cell and he was frightened that all his future held was another similar cell in the Territorial Prison. For surely if he hadn't done so already, Captain Lambert would send for the law from Griffin Creek any day now.

However, Captain Lambert had more on his mind than his reluctant prisoner. And his plan to get the ranchers to come into the safety of Fort Sherman was dashed when the surgeon told him that might not be a good idea.

'Why not?'

'Mr Fenton was at the fort today. You know, that rancher who's got a place couple of hours' ride away. Said one of his children was ill. Wanted me to go back with him to look at the boy. Said I couldn't because I've got several soldiers here who need my attention. So he asked me for some medicine. He described the boy's illness to me. He's got a high fever. It could just be a chill, or something fairly harmless, but it could be cholera or smallpox. If so, you won't want everyone gathered together in one place, exposed to infection. They'd stand more of a chance with the Indians than with cholera.'

'Hell!' Lambert said. 'You'd better go out and see as soon as you can find time.'

Dunlop nodded. 'Yes, I will.'

'It's made up my mind anyhow. My wife won't like it but Griffiths will have to take out a patrol to let the Indians know we're not about to sit back and watch while they go on the war-path.

With so much trouble brewing, Evan and Hazel were told they could no longer leave the fort and so their pleasant rides together had to come to a halt. It would hardly be the same walking around the fort where they'd be the object of the troopers' lewd curiosity.

Now, late in the evening on his way back to his quarters, Evan saw her, weeding the small vegetable garden she had laid out behind her father's house. The vegetables had to fight against the parched ground and the thriving weeds, but with Hazel's determined help were somehow growing.

'Good evening, Miss Dunlop,' he greeted her.

As she stood up, he saw that she had a streak of dirt down one cheek, making her look endearingly pretty.

'Oh, Evan, did you see Mr Fenton at the fort today? Papa says one of his children is ill. I'd like to help if I can. Will you take me out to his place tomorrow?'

Evan looked shocked. 'Of course I won't! You can't go out there!'

'Why not?'

'You know why. It could be dangerous. There might be Indians around.'

'Might, yes. Equally there might not. Despite all the rumours, no one has actually sighted any hostiles and there have been no confirmed reports of any trouble, not even down towards the Gila, let alone this side of Griffin Creek. I must go: the Fentons need help, and without it their little boy could die.'

'I refuse to let you.'

That was entirely the wrong thing to say. A stubborn look came over Hazel's face. 'Refuse? What sort of word is that? You have no right to say what I can or cannot do.'

'I'll tell your father; he'll say the same as me.'

That was an even worse thing to say. 'Oh my, what a baby you are running to my father. How dare you! I'm not a child to be told what is right or wrong. I can make up my own mind.'

'Please, Miss Dunlop, don't be so angry. I'm only saying this for your own good.'

'My well-being is nothing to do with you! And, Lieutenant, if I'm not mistaken I've had a lot more experience of the frontier than you.'

'I'm a soldier.'

'And so that makes you more intelligent and braver than me, I suppose? Next you'll be saying you're a man and I'm a woman, as if that makes me completely inferior to you!'

Evan stared at her in an agony of indecision. His mother had always put his father first. Both parents had implied that ladies did as gentlemen wished and bowed to their superior intellect. Quite clearly Hazel didn't feel the same. Instead she had a mind of her own and appeared to consider her intellect quite as good as his. He was doing this all wrong but he had no idea of how to put it right, or how to get her to see sense.

There was no way either of them could realize that part of her anger had nothing to do with what he said but was because she wanted him to hold and kiss her.

'I'm going and you're not going to stop me!'

'Please, I beg of you ...'

'Oh shut up!' Hazel said and turned on her heel, walking back to the house, outraged indignation expressed in every line of her body.

Evan sighed heavily. It was so difficult being in love. He felt sure he should tell her father what she was thinking of doing but if he did he might destroy their friendship forever. He couldn't risk that. Instead he determined to keep a very careful eye on her and make sure she didn't leave the fort. He was certain that by tomorrow she would have calmed down and would see the wisdom of his advice.

Hazel knew very well that she shouldn't have

stormed at Evan like she had. He was only worrying about her because he was concerned. She just didn't like anyone using such a patronizing tone towards her. She was nineteen and quite capable of looking after herself. But he'd meant well and when she returned from the Fentons she'd make it up to him.

She had a momentary qualm, worrying about the Indians, but surely there was no real danger; everyone knew the Apaches were unlikely to come near to the fort.

Anyway she intended to go to the ranch to see the little boy; for duty came first and Hazel took her duties as a nurse extremely seriously.

EIGHT

Lieutenant Evan Griffiths entered Captain Lambert's office and saluted smartly. 'Sir, you sent for me.'

'Yes, Lieutenant, sit down.' The young officer's earnestness always amused Lambert. A few months more and he'd become as casual as everyone else at the post, but in the meantime, Griffiths acted as if he was stationed in Washington where there were generals to impress. 'Lieutenant, I suppose you know about the whiskey trader who is also selling guns to the Apache?'

'Yes, sir.' Even Evan, who was usually one of the last to know what was happening, had heard about that.

'The prisoner, Kilkline, believes that it's probably his friend Harry Phillips who's responsible. I think it likely too. We know that the man who was with Brooks was a Southerner and from what we learned last year Phillips is a dangerous and ruthless character. It appears he gunned down one of his own men near Griffin Creek and was ready to shoot Kilkline as well. Therefore, he'd think nothing of shooting Brooks and the people he got the guns from. Now it appears that the guns have gotten through to the Apaches.'

'You want me to go after the Apaches?' Evan interrupted eagerly.

'Not exactly, Lieutenant. I want you to take a patrol and try to find out more about this trader, if he is indeed Harry Phillips; where he's operating from; how many guns he's got. Anything that can be of help in stopping him.'

'Yes sir,' Evan's eyes shone. Here was his first real chance to prove himself. He mustn't fail; he wouldn't fail!

'And if, by any chance, you do come across the trader himself, bring him in for questioning. Take Sergeant Price with you. And, Lieutenant, be careful. You are in no circumstances to engage any Indians. You will not have enough men with you to do so. This is just a reconnoitring patrol. Do you understand?'

'Yes, sir.' Evan acknowledged the order and stood up to go, just as the door opened and Captain Dunlop came in.

'Sorry sir,' he said breathlessly. 'I know you're busy but this is important.'

'What's the matter?'

'It's Hazel; she's gone!'

'Gone?' Lambert repeated. 'What do you mean?'

Evan went very red and he began to tremble. It wasn't that he'd forgotten about Hazel and her threat to leave the fort that morning. When he'd woken up he'd been determined to go and see her and, if she hadn't changed her own mind, either persuade her to do so or find some way of forcing her not to go. If it meant she hated him, better that than the risk she would run.

Then Corporal Hall had knocked with the information that the captain wanted to see him and urgently.

Evan had been in a quandary. He couldn't ignore his superior officer's order, yet what to do about Hazel? He didn't like to make one of the non-commissioned officers responsible for finding and stopping her. Hazel would most surely not like that and it wouldn't be fair on either one of them. Captain Dunlop, a late riser, wouldn't be up yet.

In the end he had decided that as it was very early, even if she was still intent on going, she wouldn't be ready to leave for quite a while yet. There was time for him to see the Captain before speaking to her.

In the excitement of being told that he was to lead an important, and possibly dangerous, patrol, Evan knew he had momentarily put her to the back of his mind. How could he? For now it appeared he'd been wrong. Oh why, why hadn't he spoken to her father last night?

Dunlop's words confirmed his fears.

'She got up early and went out. That's not unusual. Hazel is always up and doing something. I thought she'd be over at the guardhouse looking after that Rebel. But she wasn't. He hasn't seen her. I've looked for her everywhere but she's not round the post. Now Corporal Hall has told me two other troopers, Donnolly and Frost, are also missing.'

At least Hazel hadn't been so foolish as to go all by herself.

'Where could she have gone to? She knows it's dangerous to leave the fort.'

Very comfortably, Evan interrupted. 'I think I know, sir.'

Both men turned towards him, making him go red again.

Lambert barked. 'Speak up, then.'

'She's gone to the Fentons. She thought she could help their little boy.'

'How do you know?' Dunlop asked.

'She told me last night what she was going to do.'

'And you let her go? You didn't stop her when you know there's Indian trouble brewing?'

'I'm sorry, sir, I said she shouldn't. She took no notice of me.'

'She's a silly little fool and you're even worse, Lieutenant, because you at least should know better.'

'Really Lieutenant,' Lambert said, 'I'd have liked to hope you'd have sense enough to at least tell me or Captain Dunlop. You shouldn't have let her go simply because she took no notice of what you said.'

'I'm sorry,' Evan repeated and stared at the floor, feeling sorry for himself and very guilty too.

Here he was, meant to be in love with Hazel and, because he'd only been thinking of himself, he'd let her ride away and into possible danger. He wanted and deserved any punishment the captain gave him.

'And as for those two troopers, I'll have their hides when they get back!'

'Some men will have to be sent after her. And quickly,' Dunlop urged.

'Oh please, sir, let me go, please.'

'You've caused enough trouble,' Dunlop sneered but Lambert took pity on the young lieutenant, who looked near to tears.

'Wait a minute, Captain, I was already sending Mr Griffiths here out on patrol. The men are more or less ready to go. He can make a quick detour to the Fentons and detail a couple of troopers to bring Hazel safely back to the fort.'

'Is he up to it?'

'Oh yes, sir, I can do that!'

'All right,' Dunlop agreed. 'But Lieutenant you'd better pray that she's safe!'

'You may go now Lieutenant and good luck in both your missions. I'll speak to you further about this when you get back.'

'Yes sir.' And saluting both captains, Evan was only too glad to escape. He felt awful. He'd never forgive himself if anything happened to Hazel.

'I'm sure she'll be all right, Terry,' Lambert said. 'There are no reports of the Indians having come up this far.'

'I know. I can't help but worry. She's my only

child, the only close family I have left.'

'My God, Terry, what can I say? I'll see to it that these young men don't ever behave so foolishly again.'

But Dunlop, who felt like hitting out at someone, also knew he had to be fair. 'I shouldn't be too harsh on any of them. My daughter has a pretty smile and she can be very persuasive when she likes. She needs a good hiding that's what, and she'll have one when she gets back. She can be so stubborn at times.'

'Like her father.'

Dunlop acknowledged this with a slight smile. 'You know, John, I want nothing more than to return East and this is the sort of thing that makes me determined to go. Back there I'd only have to worry about boyfriends, not wild Indians.'

Lambert nodded. He knew how Dunlop felt and sympathized. Every request that Dunlop put in for a transfer had so far been denied.

'Hazel might not feel the same.'

Dunlop looked startled. 'What do you mean?'

'I was under the impression from what she's told my wife that she likes it out here.'

'But there are her studies to finish.'

'Oh yes, she still wants to become a nurse.'

'Besides she's only nineteen.'

'Quite old enough to fall in love.'

'You think she and the lieutenant ...?'

'Given the chance, Griffiths won't be a bad officer. At the moment he can't help being rather foolish and inexperienced.'

Dunlop sighed. 'Perhaps you're right. It's hard to know what to do for the best with a daughter growing up.' He said no more, feeling guilty. At least his daughter was there to grow up, unlike Lambert's son, who was so badly hurt it might have been better were he dead. He sighed. Life at times could be so hard. 'I suppose there's no way I can go with the lieutenant?'

'I wish there was, Terry, but your duty is here at the post. We have men sick, who need attention. Besides you'd be too emotionally involved.'

Dunlop reluctantly acknowledged this. Waiting was always the hard part but he'd been in the army long enough to know that waiting occupied a great deal of an officer's time.

'I'll keep you informed, Terry.'

Dunlop had no sooner gone than McPhee knocked and came in. 'Sir, permission to go with the lieutenant.'

'Denied, Private.'

'But, sir, that poor young lady might be in danger.' Despite his brutal nature, McPhee had a sentimental streak where young women were concerned, even foolish ones.

'Sergeant Price is going with the lieutenant. He's a good man.'

'Meaning I'm not?'

'Meaning that you'd find it difficult to follow orders.'

'We all know how the lieutenant feels about young Miss Hazel, that might cloud his judgement. You should forget what I done, sir, and let me do my job.'

'I'm sorry, Private, the matter is closed. Don't dare try to tell me what I should do.'

'No, sir, I'm sorry; I meant no disrespect.' McPhee left the office, disgruntled and annoyed.

Worried, Lambert watched him go. The trouble was the man was probably right, but the army rules, by which they all had to abide, meant that it was too soon to forgive him and promote him again. But McPhee knew Indians and it was a waste of a good fighter and a good leader. Not that Lambert had long to ponder on his problems, for almost at once his orderly of the day knocked on the door.

Now what? Was he never going to get any peace?

'Yes, Corporal, what is it?'

'Sir, there are two men outside, asking to see you.'

'Who are they?'

Corporal Hall wrinkled his nose in some distaste. 'Disreputable types, sir, but I think you'd better see them. Its important. It's about young Kilkline.'

Lambert sighed. 'All right, Corporal, show them in.'

NINE

'It's so good of you to come here like this, Miss Dunlop.' Mrs Fenton twisted her hands together as Hazel bent over little Charley feeling his forehead. 'I was at my wit's end. He's been poorly for days.'

'I'm pleased to help.' That was true, but all the same Hazel knew that she shouldn't have come.

The Fentons' ranch was much further from the fort than she had thought and, although they hadn't said anything, Troopers Donnolly and Frost were nervous over the fact that three people, one of whom was a woman, presented an ideal target for attack by Indians.

She would be in trouble when she got back to the fort and, worse, the two soldiers she'd sweet-talked into accompanying her would be in trouble as well; and so would Lieutenant Griffiths for not reporting her foolish intentions.

Still she didn't see what else she could have done. Poor Mrs Fenton was so worried, so grateful to Hazel for coming that getting into trouble with her father seemed a small price to pay for being able to give the woman some comfort. The girl felt very sorry for her.

Mrs Fenton couldn't be much more than thirty, yet her hair was already turning grey and her skin was brown, with wrinkles round her eyes. Hazel loved the West but she had to admit it was a harsh way of life for women whose men could hardly provide for them. And Mr Fenton looked as if he came into that category.

Not that he seemed lazy or unkind. Hazel felt sure he worked hard and wanted to do his best for his family. It was simply that in choosing to start up a small ranch out of nothing was surely not the easiest way of doing so, especially in such a hostile environment.

And the Fentons' ranch wasn't much of a place. Just a small adobe house, a corral, a vegetable garden and a few head of livestock.

As the girl's eyes strayed round the dark, barely furnished house, Mrs Fenton must have sensed what she was thinking, for she said, 'Mr Fenton and I had a farm back in New England. It was terribly hard work and the land was poor. So we decided to move out here.'

'How long ago was that?'

'Five, six years, just before the war started. We've done reasonably well. But I surely wish we were nearer Griffin Creek. I don't manage to get into town very often. I miss company. It's so lonely out here. Oh, Miss Dunlop, don't get me wrong. I love my husband and my family …'

'Don't worry.' Hazel held the woman's hand for

a moment. 'I understand. There isn't much company at the fort. Mrs Lambert is very kind, of course, but there are no girls of my own age to talk to. Once things start to get settled, more people will come here and it'll improve.'

'You think the Indian situation will ever be settled?'

Clearly the fact that at any moment the Apaches could go on the war path was the greatest worry on Mrs Fenton's mind.

'We're so isolated here. Mr Fenton says the Indians will never dare attack so near the fort but, I ask you, how would the soldiers know what was happening, or get here in time to help?

'Captain Lambert has patrols and scouts out all the time keeping an eye on the situation. I'm sure your husband is right and you have nothing to fear.'

Just then little Charley moaned and tried to sit up in bed and Hazel turned her attention to him. Nearby the other boy, Dick, watched with wide open eyes. 'Has the medicine Papa gave you helped?'

'A little. Is he badly ill?'

'He's got a fever, Mrs Fenton, but I don't think it's anything serious.'

'I was fearing smallpox or cholera.'

'It's nothing like that. Perhaps he's had a chill and then got cold or wet on top of it? Keep him warm and comfortable for a few days and he should soon recover. And make sure he has lots of water to drink. I'll come and see him again in a few days' time.' If they let me, Hazel added silently.

'Oh Miss Dunlop, thank you, you're so kind.
You've put my mind at rest. Would you and those
two young men outside like to stay for something to
eat?'

Hazel was aware there was probably very little
to spare in the household, but it wasn't that, that
made her say, 'No, we'd better be going back to
Fort Sherman.' She knew the troopers were
anxious to relinquish their care of her and she too
wanted to get back to the safety of the fort. She
had also decided that the sooner she faced up to
whatever trouble she was in, the sooner it would
be over.

With a fond look at little Charley, Hazel went to
the door, and clutching Dick's hand, Mrs Fenton
accompanied her outside.

Over by the corral, Mr Fenton was talking to
the two soldiers. They were staring not at the
horses but at some rocks on the far side of the
scrubby meadow. There was something intent
about their attitude and as they heard her
approach, Trooper Donnolly turned round, a
worried look on his face.

'What's the matter?' Hazel asked sharply.

'I don't know, Miss Hazel,' Donnolly replied.
'Probably nothing. We thought we saw some
movement over in the rocks.'

'It was likely just an animal,' Frost added.

Hazel stared across at the boulders. She could
see nothing.

'It's not Indians, is it?' Mrs Fenton cried.

Letting go of Dick, she went up to her husband, clutching at his arm. 'Please, it's not Indians.'

'There's no need for that,' Mr Fenton said, anxiety making him abrupt.

'Perhaps we hadn't better leave, not yet,' Hazel said. If there were Indians about, and like Mrs Fenton she fervently hoped there weren't, they would all be safer, staying together, in shelter. Besides they couldn't leave the Fentons to face any possible danger on their own.

'Good idea,' Donnolly agreed. 'And you'd better go inside. Take her and the kid with you.'

Before Hazel could move, a sudden wild whooping sound from the rocks stopped them all in their tracks. A whirring followed and, almost without warning, an arrow thudded into Frost's chest, picking him up, flinging him back on the ground. His scream of pain and surprise was echoed by screams from Hazel and Mrs Fenton.

'Get inside! Get inside!' Donnolly yelled. He got down on one knee and raising his carbine, let loose with several shots towards the rocks.

Fenton bent down over Frost and began to drag him to the house, but, with a little moan, the man died.

'Leave him!' Donnolly ordered. 'Get his guns!'

As Hazel frantically ushered Mrs Fenton and Dick towards the house, more arrows fell amongst the dirt of the yard, but hit nothing. She glanced at the rocks and her heart flipped over with fear. Several Indians had appeared there.

Fenton pushed his wife and Hazel into the

house and Donnolly followed, slamming the door shut behind him.

'We'll all be killed! We're going to die!' Mrs Fenton screamed.

'Come along, Mrs Fenton,' Hazel tried to comfort her. 'They won't attack when they see we're well armed.'

But Mrs Fenton refused to listen. She clutched Dick to her and started to wail.

Donnolly swung back from the window where he had been staring out. 'The bastards have got guns! It's that goddamned trader whose fault this is!' He took his service revolver from its holster and passed it to Hazel. 'Can you shoot?'

'I know how to aim and fire. I've never shot at anyone.'

'Well do it now! And for Chrissakes don't even think about it. They'll shoot you if they get the chance. Our only hope is to make them suffer so much they think twice about attacking. Mr Fenton, you take the back. Miss Hazel, you and me'll take the front.'

Hazel nodded, too scared to speak. Her heart was thumping so painfully she feared it would burst and instead of standing here, aiming and firing out of the window, what she really wanted to do was give in to hysterics like Mrs Fenton.

'And Miss Hazel,' Donnolly paused.

'Yes?'

'Save one bullet for yourself.'

TEN

Jarrod watched apprehensively as Captain Lambert came into his cell. Now what?

'Sit down, Mr Kilkline.'

Even more worried at the man's hostile tone, Jarrod sat on the edge of the bunk. Lambert pulled a piece of creased paper from his pocket and passed it to him. 'That mean anything to you?'

'Oh, God.'

It was a wanted poster. *Jarrod Kilkline –* *Wanted, dead or alive, for the murder of a Union* *Soldier, Georgia. Reward $200.*

Jarrod felt his heart and stomach sink. 'Where did you get this?'

'Is what it says true?'

'Sort of.'

'Mind explaining what that means?'

'I shot and killed a Union soldier, yeah, but only because he was on my family's property, shooting at me. It was self-defence and I was given no choice. But I don't expect you or any of your soldier friends to believe that.'

'It doesn't really matter what I believe. The only

thing that matters is that it happened and the wanted poster is genuine.'

'Where did you get it?' Jarrod repeated his earlier question.

Lambert grimaced. 'Two bounty hunters have turned up here. They say they've been looking for you for months. Evidently they nearly caught up with you in Griffin Creek but you got away from them. Is that true?'

'Yeah.' Jarrod felt even more wretched thinking of the two men who, the previous year, had confronted him on the streets of the town.

'I don't like the sort of person who becomes a bounty hunter. They're not interested in preventing crime only in collecting the reward money. But while there aren't enough lawmen around they're a necessity.'

'What are you telling me?' Suspicion dawned in Jarrod's eyes.

'They've got a wanted poster out on you. For murder. I've got no choice but to hand you over to them.'

'You can't!' Jarrod leapt to his feet. 'Look, you can see I'm wanted dead or alive. They won't want the bother of hauling me all the way back to Georgia and having to feed me, when they can turn up there with my body and claim exactly the same reward. They'll shoot me before we get a mile down the road.'

'I'm inclined to agree.'

'Well, then?'

Captain Lambert shrugged. 'There's nothing I

can do.'

'What about the stagecoach robberies? The murder of the guard?' Jarrod was suddenly much more willing to take his chances with the good citizens of Griffin Creek and the probability of a jail sentence rather than face certain death with the likes of the bounty hunters.

'The other, earlier crime takes precedence.'

'Oh, Jesus.' Jarrod sank back down on the bunk and put his head in his hands.

'I'm sorry.'

Jarrod sighed deeply. 'Sure you are.'

'They want to leave after they've eaten.'

Once Lambert had gone and the door was locked behind him, Jarrod lay down on the bunk, hands behind his head, looking at the ceiling, giving into self pity. He felt quite sure he'd never reach Georgia to face trial, but even if he did, they probably already had the rope waiting for him.

The two bounty hunters, whose names were Colin Fox and Mick Reynolds, sat eating and drinking in the sutler's store. They weren't in any real hurry. The search for their victim had come to an end at last, and they could be on their way soon enough.

They were both young men, mean looking, unshaven and in need of a wash. On the trail, they didn't bother about things like that. Fox was the elder of the two and the one who had kept the wanted poster, for Reynolds, who was slightly younger, could neither read nor write. Both carried revolvers and rifles.

They'd drifted into bounty hunting for a living, mostly because it wasn't particularly hard work and paid well. It was either work for the law or against it, and of the two this seemed preferable, involving less risks.

'Ready Col?' Reynolds drained his glass of beer. 'Ain't much to keep us here.' He'd been hoping there might be some women about the fort but, disappointed, was ready to go back to the bright lights of Griffin Creek for a couple of nights.

'Yeah, guess so. That cap'n didn't look too pleased to see us, did he?'

The two men got a similar reaction most places they went.

'Don't matter much what he thought. We ain't done nothing wrong. Kilkline is the guilty one. Let's get someone to take us to him.'

Jarrod was led from the cell by Corporal Hall, who looked no more pleased than his captain at what was happening. The two bounty hunters stood nearby, eyeing Jarrod greedily, while he stared back at them sulkily, scared too.

'Well, well, so you are Mr Kilkline,' Fox smirked. 'Thought you must be, despite how we got fooled. You've led us a real dance.'

'But we caught up with you in the end.'

Fox looked at the cuts and bruises that still marred Jarrod's face. 'Looks like someone else has saved us the bother of taming you. Pity. I was looking forward to making sure you knew you had to toe the line. Who beat you up?'

'Him.' Jarrod nodded towards McPhee, who was

standing nearby, gloating.

'Want any help, boys?' he called.

'No thanks, we can manage,' Fox replied. 'We're used to dealing with ruffians like this. Put your hands out, Mr Kilkline.' Sullenly Jarrod did so, and Fox pulled a pair of handcuffs from the belt at the back of his trousers, securing them on Jarrod's wrists.

'He don't look up to much do he?' Reynolds smirked. 'Hardly capable of all he's done.'

'All the same we ain't about to take any chances. Don't you forget that Mr Kilkline. The poster says "dead or alive". Don't matter much to us which way it is.'

'It's not something I'm likely to forget.'

'Come on then, let's get going.' Fox shoved Jarrod forward.

All round them, the usual bustle of the fort was going on. The blacksmith was shoeing a horse, the orderly was hurrying from the command post to Officers Row. Captain Lambert stood on the verandah looking across at him, or perhaps he was looking at Lieutenant Griffiths who was getting ready to ride out at the head of a patrol.

A few soldiers cast curious glances in Jarrod's direction, but mostly they took no notice.

Over by the flagpole, Lieutenant Griffiths faced the patrol. There were twenty men, plus Sergeant Price. His eye quickly ran over them and they stared back at him, hoping he wasn't about to complain that some of them weren't carrying sabres and make them go and get the useless weapons.

Fort scuttlebutt had quickly spread so that they knew that not only were they going out on patrol, hopefully to catch the renegade gun trader, but also because Miss Dunlop had gone missing. They were eager to leave so they could rescue Hazel and quite ready to blame the lieutenant for her possible peril if he did anything to delay them.

For once regulations were the last thing on Evan's mind.

'Sergeant, order the men to mount up.'

'Yes, sir.'

Evan swung up on his horse, and permitted himself a moment of pleasure as he glanced back and saw the men mount in swift, easy movements. They might bitch about having to train, but thanks to it, when the time came for action, it meant he had no need to worry about how these soldiers would behave. He raised a hand. 'Forward.'

Between Fox and Reynolds, Jarrod was marched over to the stables, where they had left their horses and where orders had been given for Jarrod's horse to be saddled and bridled.

McPhee followed them, grinning all over his face. At last the Rebel was not only getting out of his hair, but more importantly was going to get what he deserved. He only wished he could be there to see him get hung. As far as he was concerned that should be the fate of all the Southern Rebels who had dared fight against their own country.

Reynolds helped Jarrod up on to the animal, and Fox turned to him to say, 'Any nonsense, mind, and you'll end up lying face down over the saddle. Behave yourself and you might get to Georgia in one piece, cause any trouble and you'll regret it.'

'Bye Reb,' McPhee said as the three men rode by him, but Jarrod was too sunk in his own misery to take any notice.

As they rode out of the fort, Lieutenant Griffiths and his patrol started off in the opposite direction. Evan glanced across at Jarrod, wondering what was happening and where he was being taken, and then promptly forgot him. He had too much on his mind to worry about anyone else.

ELEVEN

The patrol had been riding for some time when they came to a halt for a breather at the top of a grassy knoll.

'Sir, look.' Sergeant Price pointed ahead to where a column of smoke spiralled straight up into the sky.

Evan shaded his eyes with his hand. It was definitely smoke not dust. And it was situated in the direction in which the column was headed.

'My God, Lieutenant, I think it's coming from the Fenton place! Shit, we're too late.'

Evan was too anxious, too scared, to reprimand the man for swearing. He felt like swearing himself. 'Sergeant, ensure the men are careful. There could be danger up ahead. Be ready.'

'Yes, sir.' Price needed no telling. 'But I reckon if there are Indians up ahead, they see us they'll vamoose.'

'I hope so, Sergeant.' Evan raised his arm and waved the troop into a trot and then a canter.

As the fort came into sight on the horizon, Lester Peabody heaved a sigh of relief. He was a patient man but it had been a long ride in pursuit of Jarrod Kilkline, across dusty, unending country. And while not much frightened him, he'd spotted Indian sign several times during the last few days. No way did he want to get captured by a group of Apaches on the war path.

Now he felt certain he was closing in on his prey. He couldn't have said why, it was a matter of an instinct that rarely let him down. Back in that one-horse town, Kilkline hadn't known who was after him. All he'd known was that he was suddenly running. He'd panicked, making Peabody's job of following him all that much easier.

Kilkline might not be at Fort Sherman but he was nearby and soon Peabody would be facing him over the barrel of a gun. It would then be up to Kilkline whether the trigger was pulled or not. Peabody preferred taking prisoners in alive but if they were dead it caused him no sleepless nights.

Thus, so sure he was almost at the end of his search, Peabody wasn't in the least bit pleased to learn that Kilkline had not only eluded him but was, in fact, being taken back to Georgia.

'What!' he roared in disbelief. 'You let him go with a couple of damned bounty hunters! You'd better have a damn good explanation, Lambert.'

Wondering what Mr Lester Peabody called himself, if not bounty hunter, Captain Lambert, who didn't appreciate being yelled at in his own office, replied coldly, 'They had all the necessary paperwork.'

'You must have known the bastard was wanted

for the stagecoach robberies and the murder of a guard. You should have held him for that.'

'That was precisely what I was doing. Then these two came along. The earlier crime was more important.'

'Because a soldier was involved, I suppose?'

'No. Kilkline was actually wanted for the soldier's murder. He hadn't killed the guard, only been there when it happened.'

'That's what he told you.'

'I happened to believe him.'

'Mr Thorndike won't like this.'

'I can't help that. Mr Thorndike will have to take it up with the appropriate authorities and let the law deal with it.'

Peabody looked as if he couldn't care less about a small technicality such as the law. 'Which way did they go when they left here?'

'I don't know their exact route but as their destination was Georgia, I guess they were heading for the nearest stagecoach heading east. They wouldn't want to go all that way on horseback.'

'East you say?'

'Yes. Look, Mr Peabody, you're not going to do anything stupid are you?'

'Captain Lambert, I don't know whether you'd call it stupid or not but I intend to catch up with Kilkline ...'

'And then?'

'And then me and those other fellas will just have to work out whose prisoner he really is.'

Peabody gave a grin that sent a shiver down even Lambert's hardened spine.

'I didn't ought to let you go.'

'Don't see how you can stop me. I haven't done anything wrong. I'm not under arrest, am I?'

'No.'

'Then, Captain, I'm free to go?'

Peabody obviously knew his rights. And Lambert was of the opinion that Jarrod Kilkline would stand more of a chance with Peabody than with those other two; not much of a chance admittedly, simply more of one. And he was probably more likely to get fair trial with a Griffin Creek jury than with the conquering Northern army in Georgia.

'Yes, Mr Peabody, you're free to go whenever you like.'

With Sergeant Price at his side, Evan rode up to the Fentons' place. His eyes seemed to take in everything at once but his mind didn't want to admit what he saw.

There was a dead horse in the corral, the walls of which had been knocked down, while Trooper Frost, arrow sticking from his chest, lay where he had fallen. He'd been scalped. Smoke, black and oily now, still billowed from what remained of the house. Some pieces of furniture had been taken and flung out into the yard, while the vegetable plot, so lovingly cared for by Mrs Fenton, was trampled and destroyed.

The Indians had long gone.

'Here, Lieutenant.' Along with several of the troopers, Price had dismounted, and now he called to Evan from the rear of the house.

Evan got off his horse and went over to the men, who looked shocked and angry. He soon saw why.

That was where the other bodies were.

Donnolly hadn't been as lucky as Frost. He, along with Fenton, had been tortured before he died. And body mutilated afterwards. The two small boys lay next to one another, skulls smashed, and next to them was Mrs Fenton. Her eyes were open in a horrified stare. It was clear she'd been raped before being killed.

'Jesus Christ,' Evan muttered and stumbled away behind the privy to be violently sick. He felt ashamed of himself, thinking that he should be back there giving orders, but he couldn't face what had happened. He couldn't.

No one seemed to mind. They were all horrified themselves. But they'd mostly seen sights like this before and while not used to them could at least handle them. After a while Sergeant Price came over to where Evan sat on the ground, arms around his drawn-up knees.

'Sir, I've ordered a burial detail. The bodies are covered decently now.'

'Good, thank you.' Reluctantly Evan got to his feet.

'Lieutenant.'

'Yes?' Evan was alerted by the man's worried tone.

'Well, Lieutenant, there's, er, no sign of Miss

Dunlop anywhere.'

Evan came to a startled halt. In his anger and anguish he'd momentarily forgotten all about the girl he'd come here to save.

'She's not in the house, nor anywhere close. I've had men looking. They haven't found anything.'

Evan had gone so white that Price feared he was going to faint. 'Wh … where can she be then?'

'I think,' Price replied bleakly, 'that it means the Apaches have taken her with them.'

'Oh my God! Hazel!'

'I'm sorry, sir.'

'Are you sure?'

'I can't figure out any other explanation. Where else could she have gone? She wouldn't have left without Donnolly and Frost. And if she was hiding some place she'd have revealed herself once she saw us and knew the danger was past.'

'Perhaps she's lying hurt somewhere.' But Price's face indicated he didn't think that likely. 'But why would they take her with them? Why not kill her as they did poor Mrs Fenton?'

Price shrugged. 'Who knows what it gets into an Indian's mind to do.'

'Mrs Fenton was raped wasn't she?'

'Yes, several times I should say.'

'And are they going to rape Hazel?'

'Maybe.'

'There's no need to be delicate with me, Sergeant. I know it happens.'

'Well, then, yes sir. She's a pretty young white woman. They were probably saving her until after they'd had their way with Mrs Fenton. It might be that we disturbed them before they could do so and they hightailed it out to have her at their leisure.'

'Was she made to watch what they did?'

'I expect so. They'd think that funny.'

'Sarge,' a young trooper ran up, giving Evan a sketchy salute, before hurrying on, 'Sarge, we've found tracks. Looks like there was seven or eight of the murdering red devils and they've gone west towards the hills. Don't reckon they're that far ahead of us.'

'Is there any sign of Miss Dunlop with them?'

'No, Lieutenant. But she'd be riding a horse wouldn't she? So we wouldn't be able to tell.'

'Let's go then.'

'Where?'

'After them, of course, Sergeant. If they haven't got that much of a start on us then we might catch them before they reach the hills. Before they can harm Miss Hazel.'

Price looked worried. He wished it was McPhee here and not him. He hadn't been a sergeant long and wasn't quite sure how, or whether, to argue with a commissioned officer. 'I wouldn't advise it, sir,' he said at last.

'Why not?' Evan demanded angrily. 'There are at most eight of them. There are twenty of us. We're better equipped, better fighters. Dammit man, we're United States soldiers! Are you saying we aren't a match for a bunch of savages?'

'Of course not.' Price did not like to remind the

young lieutenant that a number of other soldiers
had said the same thing, only to find out how
wrong they were. 'But we don't know whether or
not they're meeting up with a bigger bunch some
place. Supposing the whole tribe is waiting in the
hills? We could have a real fight on our hands
then.'

'And supposing they're not? I hope you're not
suggesting that I abandon Miss Hazel to a fate
worse than death?'

'No. I'm worried about her too. But I think we
oughta go back to the fort, tell the cap'n what's
happened and get help. I know we've got supplies
and plenty of ammunition with us, but not enough
if we have to follow 'em for miles. And we haven't
got a scout or a tracker with us.'

'The Indians have left us an easy trail to follow.'

'For now, yeah. And that's something else
suspicious, sir. It smells of trap to me.'

'Perhaps they're simply not bothered because
they think no one will be going after them.'

'Yes, sir, maybe you're right. But if so what
happens if the savages see us coming? If it is a
bunch of 'em on their own, they won't want to face
a superior force but will split up and make a run
for it.'

'I'm not concerned about catching the Indians
and punishing them for what they did here. I'm
only concerned in rescuing Miss Hazel. If they
know we're chasing them they won't have time to
stop and harm her. They'll run, as you say, and
leave her behind, safe.'

'I doubt that. They'd be more likely to kill her. And, sir, I know she's probably going to be raped but as for that being a fate worse than death, well maybe you'd like to ask Miss Dunlop herself whether she'd rather be alive or dead.'

'Oh God, I suppose you're right. But I can't let them reach the hills and disappear. I can't just leave Hazel. She could be relying on me.' Evan didn't know what to do. He could hardly think straight. All his instincts told him to get back to Fort Sherman and get as many men as were necessary to scare the Indians into quitting. But his heart told him he must do all he could to save Hazel. Heart overcame good sense.

'I want you to take the men back to Fort Sherman and explain matters to Captain Lambert.'

'And what about you, sir?'

'I'll take three men with me and ride after the Indians. That way we'll know where they go with very little likelihood that they'll realize they're being followed. We'll also be able to leave a trail so the captain can catch up with us quickly.'

'You can't do that!'

'Yes I can. Oh don't worry I shan't get close to them.' After seeing what had been done to Donnolly and Fenton, Evan had no wish to be in an Indian fight where he might be captured alive. 'I simply want to keep them in sight.'

'I don't know, Lieutenant, the Indians could be watching their back trail. Supposing they spot you? Four of you would be a target for them.'

Fearing he was going to be unlucky, Price went on. 'Perhaps we oughta all go back.'

'Never, Sergeant, never!'

'I don't like it.'

'It's not for you to like it or not.' Evan put on his best West Point behaviour. 'You're the sergeant, the one who takes orders, I'm the lieutenant and the one who gives them.'

'Yes, sir.' Price visibly wilted. All his determination to do what he felt best faded. If that was what the lieutenant wanted, who was he to argue?

'Ask for volunteers will you? We'll set out straightaway. I want to get the smell of this place out of my nose. And you and the others get back to the fort and bring help as quickly as you can. We'll be depending on you.'

'All right. And, sir, be careful.'

TWELVE

'Wake up.' Fox woke Jarrod by the simple expedient of kicking him in the ribs.

Jarrod groaned, opening his eyes. He'd spent the night tied to a tree, and he was cold and uncomfortable, his leg aching.

The night before when the two bounty hunters stopped and made camp, they hadn't bothered to give him anything to eat or drink. Maybe, he thought sourly, they intended to let him starve to death and save the cost of a bullet.

The camp they'd set up was sprawling and untidy, the horses picketed some way off, equipment strewn all over the ground and a large fire burning brightly. Presumably it had burnt all night for this morning it was still on the go, coffee boiling, beans and bacon frying. And while Fox and Reynolds had their rifles stacked nearby, they'd be too far away to reach quickly in any emergency.

All that despite the fact that at the fort they must have been warned the Apaches were out making trouble.

Jarrod decided he was in the hands of a couple of amateurs, who, if they didn't kill him themselves, were likely to get him killed by hostile Indians.

'Don't I get untied and given something to eat?' he said as Fox walked away. 'I didn't even have any water last night.'

The two men looked at one another and Jarrod's heart flipped over in fright. This was it! Then, with a shrug, Fox untied his arms and left Jarrod to undo the belt round his ankles.

Slowly, Jarrod got to his feet. His whole body cried out in pain from spending so long in one position. He began to stamp the circulation back into his legs, swinging his arms against his body as well as the handcuffs allowed him.

As he did so, he was aware of Fox and Reynolds whispering to one another. As their conversations were usually conducted in loud coarse tones, what they were talking about had to do with him.

Promptly, he sat down next to Reynolds so that they had to stop talking.

'That food ready yet?' Fox asked.

'Yeah.'

'Dish it up then.'

'What about him?'

'Yeah, give him some. Don't want him collapsing on us do we?' Both men laughed.

The bacon was burnt to a crisp, the beans too well done and the coffee far too strong, but Jarrod accepted both food and drink eagerly. He wasn't sure when he'd get any more and life in the unpredictable and poorly provisioned Southern army had taught him the advisability of eating as much as he could when he could.

For a while the camp was quiet as the three men concentrated on their breakfast. Afterwards, Fox and Reynolds lolled back against their saddles, rolling cigarettes. They were clearly in no hurry and Jarrod was getting more and more apprehensive by the minute.

'Jesus, I can't wait to get to Griffin Creek and have me a woman,' Reynolds sighed. 'Ain't had a woman in a long time, have we Col? what with having to chase this here sonofabitch halfway across Arizona and back.'

'Won't have long to wait now,' Fox nodded in agreement.

Jarrod was heartily fed up with listening to the pair of them going on about their love lives, or rather lack of love, which they had done nearly all the day before. Their conversation about the things they were going to delight the Griffin Creek whores by doing to them, was followed by several nods and grunts between the two men. And Fox got up to tend to the horses while Reynolds sat still, grinning.

Where was Fox? Jarrod glanced quickly round. The man was over by the horses but he'd finished feeding them and was hovering there, for no good reason.

'Can I have some more of that coffee?'

'Sure, why not?' Reynolds replied merrily. Giggling, he waved a hand towards the battered coffee-pot. 'Help yourself.'

Heart pounding, Jarrod reached over for the pot. Out of the corner of his eyes, he saw Reynolds look at Fox and give a slight nod. And Reynolds' hand dropped towards the gun.

The bastards were going to shoot him in the back!

In desperation, Jarrod made a dive for the coffee-pot. Catching hold of its handle, he swung it with all his might, crashing it against the side of Reynolds' head.

Screaming in pain and shock, the young man collapsed, hands going to his face as the boiling heat of the pot burnt his skin, feet kicking in agony. Jarrod threw the remaining contents of his mug of coffee at him as well.

'You sonofabitch!' Fox yelled and triggered off several shots, none of which struck Jarrod.

Jarrod scrambled round Reynolds, who was writhing and screaming, snatching for the bounty hunter's revolver. He got it free of the holster and rolled over on to his back.

Fox was approaching at a run, arm out-stretched, firing as he came.

Jarrod raised Reynolds' gun and shot once in reply. The bullet caught Fox in the throat and in a spray of blood the man staggered in a little dance, arms outflung, losing his grip on his revolver. He went down heavily and he didn't move again.

Breathing heavily, shaking, Jarrod stood up. Reynolds had stopped screaming and Jarrod, looking down, realized that the man was dead;

shot by one of Fox's stray bullets.

Carefully he went over to where Fox lay, kicking the bounty hunter's gun well away from him. He needn't have bothered. Fox lay on his back, eyes open to the sky, blood making an ugly wound to his throat.

Jarrod bent down by him, patting the man's pockets until he found the handcuff key. Undoing the lock, he threw handcuffs and key down beside the man.

Time to move on.

He'd been forced to leave most of his things at the fort. So now he went through the bounty hunters' saddle-bags, picking out anything that might be of use.

Not that they had much. But there was a couple of spare shirts, some socks, ammunition for a revolver and a rifle, canteen of water and some supplies of bacon and coffee. He'd also take the skillet and the coffee-pot that had saved his life. The rest he'd have to leave. While it would be handy to load it all up on one of the two spare horses, he wanted to travel fast. A pack horse would only slow him down.

He saddled and bridled his own animal. As he mounted it, he spared a glance for Fox and Reynolds. Should he bury them? His conscience told him that it seemed only right to do so, but they'd never have given him the same decency. They'd have wrapped his body in a canvas sack and carried it all the way across to Georgia without thought of a Christian burial. And supposing someone – Indians or an army patrol – had heard the shooting and were about to investigate?

No, he didn't dare hang around. So putting his guilt to one side, Jarrod dug heels into his animal's side and rode away.

Lester Peabody heard the sound of shots in the far distance just as he was packing up his meagre camp, in order to set out on Kilkline's trail once more. It could mean only one of two things: Indians or the bounty hunters. To his experienced mind it didn't sound like Apaches. There was only one gun being fired – and then suddenly another shot – the final one.

It had to be to do with Kilkline. But what? Had the bastards shot him? What did that last shot mean? Not that it mattered all that much if they had killed him. That only meant taking a dead, rather than live, body away from them.

Peabody got a move on.

He knew he was going to find something dead, even before he got to the bodies, because buzzards were circling lazily in the warm air above the desert. They told him in which direction to go and it wasn't long before he came to the deserted camp and the two dead men.

Slowly he got off his horse and studied the ground.

'So, Mr Kilkline, you're more determined and dangerous than I had you figured,' Peabody said out loud. 'And,' – he raised his head – 'where have you gone now?'

The man stood in the middle of the camp, hands on hips.

Kilkline's trail would probably be fairly easy to follow, at first anyway. All he'd want to do would be to get away from the vicinity of the fort and he wouldn't be too concerned about hiding his tracks. Peabody could either go after him or bury these two and take their horses back to the fort and let them know there what had happened.

He badly wanted to go after Kilkline. He didn't like being led a merry chase and to so nearly have caught up with him and then to lose him, yet again, was galling to a man of Peabody's experience. It didn't look good.

Yet there was the Indian question.

Before he'd left Fort Sherman, a sergeant and part of an earlier patrol had come back, covered in dust and sweat, to pour out a tale about a local rancher and his family being attacked and killed.

That meant the hostiles were in the vicinity and could even be attracted to the scene of shooting. He had no wish to tangle with them.

For about the first time in his career, Lester Peabody was undecided as to what to do.

THIRTEEN

The Indian trail led straight towards the distant blur of the hills. There was no sign of the Apaches and the valley floor was quiet, the only beings moving the four soldiers.

Private Cherry rode by Evan's side, the two others close behind. They were all muttering about the pace he set, about the fact that he'd hardly allowed them any rest the night before and the fact that they might be riding all alone into danger. Evan had asked for volunteers to accompany him. None had been forthcoming so these three had been ordered into the duty by Sergeant Price and they weren't very happy.

'Sir,' Cherry ventured. 'Sir, I think we oughta rest.'

'Not yet, Trooper.'

'It's very hot and uncomfortable, sir.'

'And even more uncomfortable for Miss Dunlop. It's her we should be thinking about, not ourselves.'

'Yes sir,' Cherry agreed miserably and with one look at his superior officer's face, lapsed into resigned silence.

Fearing mutiny, Evan allowed a short stop for a noon break but anxious to be on his way, it wasn't long before he ordered them back into the saddle.

It was hot, even so early in the year, the sun was shining in an almost cloudless sky. The landscape was arid, seemingly flat, broken here and there by tall buttes and strangely shaped cactus, the only other vegetation the ever present sagebrush and some stunted mesquite trees.

The horses plodded along, heads down, little spurts of dust rising up beneath their hooves. The men slept in their saddles and Evan too found his eyes irresistibly closing, head falling forward to his chest.

He jerked his head up. They were nearing the foothills: line upon line of ever higher saw-toothed hills, covered with scrubby grass and trees, outcrops of rocks visible among the pines. And half a mile or so before them stood a small grove of cypress trees, perhaps indicating a waterhole. They could rest there for the remainder of the afternoon in welcome shade and travel on again when cool evening came.

'Look lively,' he said and turned towards the two men riding behind him to make sure they had heard.

As he did so Cherry cried out in fright. Swinging back he saw that from out of nowhere several Indians had sprung into view and were firing at them.

'Christ!' Evan yelled and tried to pull his sabre

free of its scabbard, as well as controlling his
horse which was rearing in fright. 'The trees. Get
to the trees!' He had the sabre out at last and he
charged forward, scything the air with the
weapon but not hitting anything.

Someone screamed and he glanced back seeing
a soldier tumbling from his horse. The horse was
also hit and went down. Evan paused but both
man and animal were overrun by Indians too
quickly for him to do anything.

'Come on, sir, you can't help him,' Cherry
grabbed at the reins of Evan's horse.

They had just reached the shelter of the trees
when Evan felt something strike him hard in the
arm. Grunting he fell forward over the saddlehorn
and to his amazement, slid gracefully off the horse
to land on his side in the dust.

'Sir! Sir!' Cherry raced back for him and pulled
him to his feet. Together the two young men
staggered to the trees where they collapsed
behind the third soldier, who was firing towards
the gathering Indians.

'You badly hurt, Lieutenant?'

Evan looked down at the wound. There was a
lot of blood and part of his arm felt numb but he
didn't think anything vital had been struck. 'I'll be
all right.'

'Doesn't matter much anyway. We're going to be
killed.' Cherry ducked as a furious ricochet
whined off a nearby tree trunk.

'Nonsense. They won't dare attack us now we've
got cover.'

But it seemed that Evan was wrong. The rest of the Apaches had finished whatever they were doing to the trooper and the horse and had now joined their colleagues. They lay down on the ground and showed no sign of giving up and going away, while others brought up horses.

'They're getting ready to charge!'

Evan's mind was a confusion of jumbled frightened thoughts. Where had the Indians come from? One minute the desert was empty, the next filled with screaming savages intent on taking their scalps.

'What are we going to do, Lieutenant?' Cherry asked.

'What can we do but fight? Surrender is not an alternative. We've got plenty of ammunition. As long as we're careful, it should last until help arrives. Captain Lambert and his patrol could be close enough to hear the firing and if so they'll come quickly. We'll be all right as long as the Indians think they've got plenty of time and don't attack us. And surely they won't do so when they know we have superior weapons and can use them accurately.' Evan was speaking as much for himself as his men's morale.

'They seem to have done all right so far,' Cherry muttered.

'Here come the bastards!'

And suddenly, despite Evan's hopeful predictions, the Apaches were charging the position, some on foot, some on horseback.

'Fire!' Evan gave the order but he only got off

one shot before the Indians on foot dropped to the ground and disappeared and the riders peeled off. 'Where the hell have they gone?' he asked in disbelief.

'My pa always used to say that whenever you couldn't see an Apache that was the time the red bastard was about,' Cherry said. 'I didn't believe him till now. Did you get anyone, sir?'

'Don't think so.'

Several shots rang out and the other soldier was hit.

Firing in the direction he thought the Indians were, Evan scrambled back to the man. 'Oh God, he's dead,' he said and he and Cherry looked at one another in anguish.

Whooping voices came from beyond the trees and the Indians attacked again, riding up and down in front of the copse, firing steadily, lying against their horses' backs so they presented no target.

'Shoot the horses,' Evan cried.

But even when a horse went down, the Indian on its back merely dropped to the ground and scuttled away, to join in the general firing at the two remaining soldiers.

'We're going to die, ain't we, sir?'

'It certainly looks that way, Cherry.' And Evan could only wonder at his calmness. Perhaps that was what West Point training was all about: the ability to die well.

Jarrod had decided to head for the hills, hoping there to lose the pursuit he was sure would come after him. He was crossing the valley, the hills nearby, when he heard the sound of firing from some way away and then saw in the distance a grove of trees. Several Indians were riding round in front of it, pinning someone down.

Carefully Jarrod rode forward round the base of a butte, where he hid, in order to see what exactly was going on. Not that the Indians were taking any notice of him. They were much too intent on their attack. He caught a glimpse of blue uniform and grinned. Yankee soldiers.

Well no way was he going to risk life, limb or recapture for Yankee bluecoats. No sir! He was going to give this fight a wide berth. He jigged his horse into a trot, not wanting to do anything that might attract attention to himself and rode in a circle towards the hills.

Every now and then he glanced across at the trees. The fight wasn't going to last much longer, the firing from the defenders getting less and less frequent. There was probably only a couple of them alive now. Pity that sonofabitch McPhee wasn't among them.

Turning his head away, Jarrod urged his horse up the first slope of the hill. It wasn't long before they reached the top. There he pulled the animal to a halt.

'Goddammit!' he swore out loud.

And Jarrod swung his horse's head round, dug heels into its side and rode it at a gallop down the slope, back towards the trees.

* * *

The charge at a full out gallop took Jarrod back to the first heady days of the war, when Southern cavalry was invincible and it had looked like the South would win. As he rode he effortlessly drew the rifle from its scabbard, raised it and fired, at the same time letting out a Rebel yell that was quite as loud and frightening as the Indians' whoops.

As he got nearer the trees his excitement died and he thought he'd probably made the worst mistake of his life. There was only one Yankee left alive. And while he was on his knees firing steadily he wasn't preventing the Apaches from getting ever closer. Jarrod was going to die for a damn Yankee soldier.

But it was too late to change his mind. The Indians were already alerted to his presence and several were turning in his direction. While they were cautious, wondering who he was and where he'd come from, once they found out he was alone, it wouldn't take them long to rally against him.

Out in the open that would be disastrous. Jarrod had to get to the trees. But it wouldn't do much good to stay amongst them with the Yank. He'd be pinned down as well. Jarrod raised his eyes to the hills. There was where the most safety lay.

He urged his horse faster and fired point blank at the nearest Indian who fell to the ground.

Somehow his headlong charge took Jarrod through the surprised Apaches and he entered the shelter of the trees. Bent low over his animal's back, branches snatching at him, he headed straight for the Yankee.

'Get on! Get on!' he yelled and shoving the rifle back in its scabbard, reached down and grabbed at Evan's arm.

Evan clutched Jarrod's sleeve and in a blur of movement he was swung up behind his rescuer.

'Grab hold!' Jarrod caught up the reins of one of the army horses.

Yells and bullets following them, they crashed through the trees to the far side of the grove and were out in the open again. And there, Jarrod thought he heard an answering Rebel yell. No, he had to be mistaken. Or else the Indians were good mimics.

Because the Apaches had concentrated their fire on Evan at the front of the grove of trees there was no one here at the rear. It meant they had a few minutes start and the hills weren't that far away.

'Keep 'em occupied,' Jarrod said and concentrated on urging the horses into a gallop.

For a while, a couple of Indians gave chase but after Evan had fired at them, and after it was soon obvious that their small ponies were not so fast nor had so much stamina as those they were chasing, they lost heart and gave up. By the time Jarrod and Evan got amongst the pine trees they were alone.

Halfway up the hill, Jarrod pulled the horses to a halt and Evan slid to the ground, breathing heavily.

Gone was the parade-ground soldier. His uniform was torn, hat disappeared, and there were streaks of dirt and what looked suspiciously like tears down his face.

'You're wounded.' Jarrod dismounted.

Evan stared down at his arm. In the excitement of the fight and the fear of thinking he, like his men, was about to die, he had forgotten all about getting shot. Now he suddenly realized that his arm hurt. There was blood all down his jacket sleeve and his shirt was sticky and wet.

Jarrod helped Evan off with his shirt, from which he tore a strip, soaking it with water from the canteen, and bathing Evan's arm with it. Once the blood was washed away, it was possible to see that the bullet wound was only a deep jagged graze across the outside of his arm. 'It doesn't look too bad. There's no bullet in it. You were lucky. But it had better be bandaged up.'

Tearing another strip off Evan's shirt, Jarrod tied it tightly around the wound, knotting it untidily in place. 'That should do.'

Rather miserably Evan looked at his ruined shirt.

From the saddle-bags, Jarrod took one of the shirts he'd stolen from the two bounty hunters. It wasn't very clean and it was too big for the slim lieutenant but it would do. He threw it across to Evan.

'Thanks. Thanks for all your help.'

It was on the tip of Jarrod's tongue to say 'My

pleasure' but that, he felt, was going a bit too far when it was a Yankee soldier he'd saved.

'Where are all your men?'

Evan gulped down some water. 'I got them all killed.'

'What all of them?'

'There were only four of us.'

Jarrod was puzzled. 'I saw twenty or so of you leaving the fort.'

'I know. I sent most of them back.'

'What for?'

'Because the Fentons were killed and the Indians, goddamn them, had taken Hazel with them. I was going to rescue her. And now look at the mess I've made of everything! I don't deserve to be a lieutenant.'

Jarrod cast a glance down the hill. The Indians were leaving. They'd killed a couple of soldiers, got horses and guns, and were satisfied. 'The Indians have Hazel Dunlop with them?' he said bleakly, unbelievingly.

Evan nodded miserably. 'And that was all my fault as well.'

'You'd better tell me what happened.'

Quickly Evan finished his tale of woe.

'I should have stopped her from going. She's in danger because of me.'

'Well, yeah, I guess so but it's not all your fault, Miss Hazel is obviously a young woman with a mind of her own. What are you going to do now? Go back and join up with your cap'n's patrol?'

'No.'

'No? Why not?'

'Because the patrol is probably still hours behind.' Evan knew only too well how slowly the army moved, even when it was in a hurry. 'By the time they catch up, the Indians could be anywhere. Maybe even on their way to Mexico where Captain Lambert can't follow them. I'm right on their trail and I don't care about the illegality of crossing a border.'

'But look what's happened. You were attacked, nearly killed!'

'That was because we were out in the open where the Apaches could see us. Now I'm in the hills and I shall be more careful. They won't be expecting me to still be following them and I'll keep far enough back so they won't see me but when they get to wherever they're going and think they're safe then I shall be there to rescue Hazel.'

'It seems to me you want to be a hero to that little girl.'

Evan went red, because that wasn't so very far from the truth.

'It's not a very sensible thing to do.'

'I don't see as it's any of your business. I know what my duty is and I shall do it.'

'Good for you.'

'I can manage quite well on my own, so you can go your own way now.'

This sentiment was obviously not true. Evan wouldn't last five minutes out here all alone. But why should Jarrod care? The lieutenant was a soldier and a Yankee, and if he couldn't look after himself that wasn't Jarrod's responsibility. Jarrod had his own skin to save and chasing after a band of wild Indians probably wasn't the best way of going about it. Even if the lieutenant had rescued him from the boots of Sergeant McPhee, they were now all square. He owed him nothing.

But Jarrod's conscience nagged. Miss Hazel Dunlop had nursed him day and night until he was better. What was happening to her, how was she feeling?

Not so very long ago, someone Jarrod loved had been kidnapped by Harry Phillips. All he'd wanted to do was save her, no matter how or at what cost. He could understand how the lieutenant felt.

'Well?' Evan said belligerently. 'What are you waiting for?'

'I'm going with you.'

FOURTEEN

'I saw you being taken away from the fort by a couple of men didn't I?'

'Yeah, that's right.'

'Were they from Griffin Creek?'

'No.'

'And you got away from them?'

'Something like that.'

One look at Jarrod's face made Evan decide not to ask any more questions. He didn't want to know the truth because if he did he might have to do something about it.

Here he was sitting opposite a Southerner, who'd fought in the war, and who was now a wanted outlaw on the run. His mother would be horrified if she knew, his father tell him it was his duty to arrest him. Yet this same young man had saved him when he had no need to do so and was helping him now. Jarrod Kilkline might not have much idea about scouting, or the lay of the terrain, but Evan admitted, he had a lot more idea than Evan about surviving in the wilderness.

They were sitting on opposite sides of a tiny fire,

the flames crackling in the cool night air and had just finished eating a rabbit that Jarrod had shot earlier. They'd made camp in a small clearing where there was plenty of grass for the two horses and shelter for themselves.

Evan noticed that Jarrod kept rubbing his leg as if it hurt him, but he didn't like to say anything about it in case Jarrod was embarrassed.

Since their first exchange of words, apart from giving out necessary orders, Jarrod had said very little. He'd ridden out in front, not once turning his head to see if Evan was behind him. Evan was a bit scared of him and thought he didn't like him much. But now they were a bit more relaxed, his curiousity about the South got the better of him and he forced himself to make conversation.

'You fought in the war didn't you?'

'Almost from the beginning.' Jarrod lay back against a rock, looking up at the stars.

'I wish I'd been old enough to fight.'

'No, you don't. It wasn't glorious or good. It was dirty and muddy and a hard slog with the occasional fight when there was death and noise ...' Jarrod came to a halt. 'It still gives me nightmares.'

'But you wished you'd won?'

'Sure I do. I believed, and still do, in the cause and in States' rights.'

'So much so that you and your friends were willing to try and start up a new Rebel army?'

Jarrod frowned. 'That was just foolishness. It could never have happened. And while I thought that we were robbing and stealing for the South, Harry Phillips was doing it out of greed. I hope that you don't believe he's a friend of mine any more. You know, Lieutenant, I never meant for any of this to happen. I didn't expect to find myself out here in Arizona wanted by the law. When I returned from the war, I first went home to Georgia and even though my folks were dead and the farm in ruins I intended to try and make a go of it.'

'What happened?'

'The Yankee army didn't let me.'

'Oh.'

'That's what made it worse. It was bad enough losing and Lee surrendering, but finding that the North was out to ruin the South made me so mad I was willing to follow anyone who wanted to change things back to the way they were. It took a girl to make me see how wrong and stupid I was and by then it was too late. But it doesn't matter now. That part of my life has gone forever.'

'Maybe you can sort things out.'

'Yeah, maybe.' Jarrod sounded doubtful. 'What about you? Where you from?'

'Near New York.'

'And what made you go to West Point?'

'Soldiering is in my family's blood. One of my ancestors fought in the American Revolution and since then a member of each generation has fought for his country. And died too.' Evan sounded proud.

'And did you want to become a soldier as well, or was it forced on you by tradition?'

'It was what I wanted of course. And I asked to be

sent out here to the frontier rather than go to Washington and impress the generals, which my parents saw as the way to rapid promotion. This was where all the excitement and glory was. Still,' Evan grimaced, 'maybe you're the one who's right. After the last couple of days there doesn't seem much of either in fighting Indians. I was terrified.'

Jarrod grinned. 'You aren't the only one. But you get used to it. You fight and then you worry afterwards. I guess at the moment you're willing to do just that.' Remembering some of what Hazel had told him about Evan's reluctance to be anything other than strictly polite, he added, 'Are you acting out of duty or would you like Hazel to be your girl?'

Evan was glad of the darkness so that his companion, who seemed so much more worldlywise than him, even if he was only a couple of years older, couldn't see him blush. 'Yes I would. But I hope I'd be doing this for anyone.'

'I expect you would.'

Evan quickly changed the subject. 'What I can't understand is how or why the Apaches attacked us.'

'They were well armed weren't they?'

'Oh yes, with guns that seemed to range from muzzle loaders to old-fashioned single shot revolvers. They must have been supplied by your friend, er, I mean, Phillips. They also had horses.'

'Well I guess the Indians had stolen them from the Fentons or some other families they'd dealt with in the same way.'

'I know that. But Apaches,' Evan was anxious to display some knowledge and not appear a complete fool, 'usually fight on foot and use their ill-treated ponies either for escape or food. And, it's even more unusual for seven or eight Apaches to take it into their heads to attack four US soldiers. They like odds much more in their favour. It seems to me that someone must have been there, leading them, urging them on.'

Jarrod's eyes darkened. 'Harry Phillips.'

'Would he really do something like that?'

'Yeah.'

'Then he must be stopped.'

'I agree. But that, Lieutenant, might be easier said than done. Now we'd better get some sleep. Make an early start in the morning.'

'All right. And, Mr Kilkline, thanks. I don't know why you're helping me, considering I'm a Yankee soldier, but I'm sure glad you are.'

For the next few days, Jarrod and Evan followed on behind the Apaches. Up in the hills it was cold, especially at night, snow on the highest points and ice on the edges of the creeks. But once down on the other side, it soon started to get hot again. The desert was a never-ending brown, stretching ahead of them right to the border.

They didn't have the Indians in sight but kept well back, out of sight themselves, following in the general direction the Apaches were going. They left as clear a trail as they could in the hope that the army patrol would catch up with them; or at least that was Evan's hope. Jarrod had made up his mind that at the first appearance of another blue uniform he was going to hightail it out of sight as fast as he could.

Gradually, as they rode along together, the two young men forgot about being enemies. Jarrod unbent far enough to call Evan by his Christian name and to his surprise discovered that he enjoyed the company of someone who not so long before he would have termed a Yankee bluebelly and been prepared to hate.

Evan was just like himself, a young man, a long way from home, with the same hopes for the future and the same worries and fears about the present. It was a lesson he should have learned a long while ago.

At first it seemed the Indians were heading for the Gila River and then they turned off towards the Chiricahua Mountains.

'That's strange,' Evan said. 'I thought they'd go into Mexico and hide there until all this has died down.'

'Perhaps having guns makes all the difference to them.' Jarrod wished he knew a bit more about the ways and mind of an Apache. 'Or it could be Phillips playing games again.'

There was no sign of Hazel amongst the group they were following and Jarrod was scared that the Indians had already killed her and left her body somewhere. Not that he said so to Evan; it would have made no difference anyway, Evan would still have insisted on going after them. But he had the feeling from Evan's worried face that he feared much the same.

'Look!' Evan pulled his horse to a halt and pointed further along the arroyo they had just descended to get to the trickle of water in the bottom.

'What is it?' And then Jarrod too saw what had attracted the young lieutenant's attention.

A wagon stood on a rocky outcrop, two horses in the water drinking.

'Do you think it's the trader's?'

Jarrod got hold of his rifle. 'I don't like it, whoever it belongs to. What's it doing way out here? It can't belong to a settler.'

Evan rode a little closer. 'There's no sign of anyone. No camp or anything. Perhaps the owner has been killed? No, that's not right,' he answered his own question, 'the Indians would have taken the horses.'

Jarrod looked up and down the arroyo. No one, nothing, except the wagon. All his instincts told him to get away but Evan was already moving towards it. 'Careful.'

'Just a quick look. If it is the trader's and we can get his guns it could save more bloodshed.'

Cautiously they dismounted and went up to the wagon. There was no sound, not even a breath of wind.

'Cover me.' Revolver in hand, Evan climbed up on to the front of the wagon and peered inside. He let out the breath he'd been holding. The wagon was empty, no one waiting in ambush inside.

Empty except for an untidy bed, a chest and a few other bits and pieces. He climbed inside and a few minutes later emerged. 'No guns.'

'Someone clever enough to be trading to the Indians wouldn't have the guns on show for all to see. What about a secret hiding place in the bed of the wagon?'

'Maybe.'

Jarrod began to tap along the side of the wagon and to peer underneath it. He was just emerging when something cold dug him hard in his neck and a familiar voice said, 'Don't move any too quickly or you could get your damnfool head shot off.'

Slowly Jarrod stood up and turned round. He went cold with fright. Evan was being held some way away by a young Indian and another Indian held a rifle on Jarrod. While they were bad enough, it was the third figure standing nearby, hands on hips, who caused Jarrod the most fear.

'Hallo Jarrod,' he said.

It was Harry Phillips.

FIFTEEN

'Drop the rifle and slowly take your revolver out,' Phillips ordered. 'I'm sure you won't try anything stupid but if you should then the Yank lieutenant there gets hurt.'

Jarrod glanced at Evan, who grimaced at him. Evan probably expected Jarrod to do something to get them out of this mess but he couldn't do anything, but what he was told, not with the second Indian breathing down his neck and Phillips ready to carry out his threat.

Moodily he put the rifle on the ground then reached for his revolver. As he pulled it out of the holster, the Indian snatched it from him and stuck it in the concho shell belt round his waist.

Grinning, causing the scar down the side of his face to twist lopsidedly, Phillips strolled up to Jarrod. The man was in his early thirties with blue, hard eyes that glittered with excitement. His once neat and tidy hair was now long and curled, while his thick moustache hadn't been trimmed for some while. He was wearing buckskin trousers and a fringed buckskin shirt and high topped moccasins.

'Gone native have you?' Jarrod sneered.

Phillips grinned again. 'It makes me more acceptable to the Indians. And it's comfortable too. By the way meet my friends, Bull and Young Moon. They hate most white men. Luckily for me, we understand each other. They know I can show 'em a good time. We met in one of the camps when I was with Bill Brooks selling whiskey. They quickly agreed to join me.'

Jarrod wasn't surprised. The two Indians were both young men, of medium height with barrel chests. Their black hair hung to their shoulders, held in place with colourful strips of cloth. They had thin slits of mouths and mean eyes; just the type of men Phillips would join up with.

'And they helped you kill both Brooks and the Barnes family?'

'You know, Jarrod, how I can't stand fools and poor old Brooks was surely one of those. As for the Barnes, they simply got what they deserved, just like everyone does who gets in my way, sooner or later.' Jarrod took that for a threat.

'I didn't know you could speak Apache. How do you get them to do what you want?'

'Oh in my travels I've learnt one or two useful words. Otherwise we get by with a mixture of Spanish and sign language. Maybe a couple of wild Apache bucks ain't the best of travelling companions but they're surely better than you, travelling with a Yank bluebelly. I thought you'd have better taste.' Phillips cast a contemptuous glance at Evan. 'He's the one you rescued over the other side of the hills, ain't he?'

'So you were there?'

'Yeah. I recognized you all right. Did you hear my good old Rebel yell in reply? I couldn't understand why you wanted to help a Yank until I remembered that you'd forgotten your Southern upbringing and turned traitor. And now you're out here with him following the Apaches. Me and my two friends peeled off from the main bunch because we couldn't keep up with them, having the wagon, and that's when we spotted you. We've kept you in sight for days. That's why we set a trap and naturally you pair of idiots fell into it. What we couldn't make out was why you were doing what you were. Is it to do with the guns?'

'No. We're looking for a white woman we think the Indians have got.'

'Ah, ever the Southern gentleman riding to the rescue of a fair damsel,' Phillips mocked.

'Is Hazel, Miss Dunlop, with them?' Evan asked.

'You'll soon find out. It'll be quite a pleasure seeing how Apaches deal with a live Yankee soldier. Most they get their hands on are dead. I might pick up some ideas.' Phillips turned back to Jarrod.

And Jarrod knew that, however much Phillips hated United States soldiers, he'd make sure the Indians reserved their worst and most refined torture for him. He had to be punished for what Phillips' twisted mind saw as his betrayal.

'You know, Jarrod, it's good to meet up with you again. The last time I saw you, you were unconscious, tied up and waiting for me to come and kill you. Somehow you got away but not this time.'

'That's funny Harry. Because the last time I saw you you were hightailing it out of Griffin Creek as fast as you could go, scared shitless you were going to get shot.'

Phillips' eyes hardened. 'Don't get cocky with me.'

He said something to the Indians and Evan was pushed to the ground, Young Moon putting a foot on his neck. Phillips sauntered over to the wagon, reached inside and emerged with a coil of rope which he threw at Jarrod.

'Tie his wrists behind his back and his ankles together and then tie his hands and feet together. And tightly.'

Soon Evan was trussed up, hardly able to move.

When Jarrod had finished to Phillips' satisfaction, Harry swung an arm, catching him on the side of his head, knocking him to the ground. And Jarrod too quickly found himself tied up in the same way.

Both of them were slung into the wagon. The horses were hitched up, Jarrod's and Evan's animals tied to the rear of the wagon, and Phillips climbed up on to the seat. He looked back at his prisoners and whistled a few bars of 'Dixie', before setting the horses into motion. 'Won't be long now, boys.'

'Oh God, Jarrod, what are we going to do?' Evan whispered.

'I don't see as there's anything we can do, not for the moment anyhow.'

And so, tied tightly and awkwardly, bounced around on the floor of the wagon, given nothing to eat or drink, Jarrod and Evan were taken to the Indian camp in the middle of the Chiricahua Mountains.

'There you are,' McPhee put another bottle of warm beer down on the table in front of Lester Peabody. He lowered his bulk into the chair and drank half of his own beer in a noisy slurp. 'So you lost this Kilkline?'

'Yes.'

The two men were commiserating with one another's troubles in the sutler's store, part of which was set aside as a place where the troopers could drink and play cards when not on duty. Normally McPhee wasn't the type of man Peabody associated with, but this wasn't a normal time. Peabody was in danger of failing and he didn't like that.

'I intend to go after him again, when I can.'

'Damn Reb,' McPhee nodded in agreement.

'I don't care about his political persuasion, only that he broke the law.'

McPhee looked at his companion, eyes glazing over slightly, because he didn't understand all of what the man said.

'When do you think the Indian troubles will be over?'

'Who knows with Apaches? Hold on.' McPhee

had heard sounds from outside. Hoofbeats, the clink of harness and the shouts of men. It was the patrol coming back.

'They're back quickly.'

'Yeah, I ain't surprised. They went ill prepared, thinking that they'd find the lieutenant and the girl without any trouble.'

'Perhaps they have.'

'I doubt it.'

Followed by Peabody, McPhee went outside into the warm evening air. The weary looking men had dismounted in the parade ground and were leading the horses to the stables. McPhee's eyes quickly ran over them. He wasn't surprised that there was no sign of the lieutenant or of the foolish girl, who was responsible for all this. Matters to do with the wily Apache were never that easy. Captain Dunlop was gesticulating wildly at Captain Lambert and Lambert tiredly shook his head and turned away, going into the headquarters building. Dunlop remained looking at him, before walking away.

'McPhee,' Corporal Hall, who was orderly of the day, approached from headquarters. 'Cap'n wants to see you.'

'What for?' McPhee naturally didn't bother with a salute or the word 'Corporal'.

'I reckon you're going to get your stripes back.' Hall was disgruntled. Things surely had been a lot quieter without McPhee bossing everyone around, even if he hadn't behaved like an ideal private.

'Sit down,' Lambert said when McPhee presented himself. He ran a hand over his eyes. They'd been out for several days, getting nowhere, and discovering nothing except for the mutilated bodies of three more men. Of Evan Griffiths there was no sign. 'It appears he had help,' Lambert explained to McPhee. 'But who helped him I don't know. The lieutenant escaped from an Indian ambush and then with another man headed for the hills. The Apaches didn't bother to give chase. They went for the desert. And somehow we lost 'em all.'

'Why didn't the lieutenant come back here?'

'I don't know. Just wait till he does get back. There will be some harsh words said about duty and danger and behaving sensibly.'

It was the first time Lambert had ever criticized a fellow officer in front of McPhee and neither knew who was the most embarrassed.

To cover up the lapse, McPhee quickly said, 'What about Miss Dunlop?'

'Nothing. I can only presume that the poor girl is indeed with the Apaches. How has Captain Dunlop been taking it?'

'Poorly, sir. He's torn between fearing his daughter is dead and hoping that she is.'

'I can't say I've ever believed that nonsense about it being better for a white woman to kill herself rather than be taken by Indians.'

'I don't think Captain Dunlop believes it either. It's just difficult for him to imagine what's happening to Miss Dunlop and what's going through her mind. Mrs Lambert has been looking after him, sir.

'Good, good.' Lambert nodded.

His eyes began to close, jerking open again, as McPhee asked, 'Where do you think the Indians were headed?'

'The Gila, the Chiricahuas or Mexico. Take your pick. I'm hoping the scouts will pick something up. They're still out looking. And I want you to take out a patrol, find the scouts and then find Lieutenant Griffiths.'

'Me, sir?'

'Yes, you. Against my better judgement and solely for the sakes of the lieutenant and Miss Dunlop, I'm reinstating you to the rank of sergeant.'

McPhee beamed. This was his proper role in life. A leader of the men. 'Thank you, sir.'

'Don't let me down McPhee. Because if you do I'll have you busted back to private so fast you won't see it happening.'

But they both knew it was an empty threat.

SIXTEEN

'Nearly there now,' Phillips said cheerfully as the wagon rattled up a steep incline. 'Sorry you're being jostled around so much, you must be getting bruised.'

'Like hell you're sorry,' Jarrod muttered. Up till then, he had felt too tired, too hungry and thirsty, and too uncomfortable to be scared. Now, knowing they were almost at the Indian village, his guts churned and he wondered if he was going to be sick. Apaches. From the days of his youth he'd heard tales of the atrocities they committed upon their white captives. He couldn't imagine what it must be like to hurt so much death was a welcome release. He glanced across at Evan. The lieutenant was very pale but he managed a weak smile.

Before long the wagon came to a halt. The back was lowered and Jarrod was dragged out and flung to the ground. The rope tying his arms and legs together was slashed and he was pulled to his feet. He stood swaying, disorientated, arms feeling like they were on fire. Beside him he heard Evan groan and couldn't decide whether it was with pain or fear.

The Indian village was situated halfway up the side of the hill, along a path so steep and rocky the wagon couldn't get up it. It wasn't much of a place. Just a few grass wickiups situated around a small open area. The huts had a look of impermanence as if they had just been put up and could just as easily be taken down. Off to one side was a brush corral housing some ponies and mules. What made the camp so secure was its situation. High up in the mountains, surrounded by rocks and trees, with only one approach and that so narrow not more than one rider could go up it at a time, it was virtually impregnable.

Free of their bonds, Jarrod and Evan were pushed forward. Soon the presence of the newcomers was spotted. Gradually all the Indians in the camp – warriors, old men, women and children – came to the edge of the clearing to watch. They were ominously quiet.

Amongst them was a tall man with broad shoulders and a wide chest. He stared at the two prisoners with an intelligent gleam in his dark eyes. He was good looking with a straight nose, high forehead and thick black hair.

'Oh my God,' Evan whispered. 'That's Cochise himself.'

'Too right Lieutenant,' Phillips agreed.

Jarrod was surprised. According to what he'd heard, Cochise was a great chief, yet this man was dressed simply, with nothing gaudy about him, unlike some of the other braves. But looking at him, Jarrod could see he had a quiet dignity that made him different to the rest.

'I thought he was having one of his attempts at staying peaceful,' Evan said.

'He was until I came along selling guns. What self-respecting Indian could resist such an offer? After all with guns the white advance can be brought to a halt.'

'You know that's not true.'

'Ah, I do, Jarrod, ol' son. Cochise don't.'

'And it doesn't matter to you that both Indians and whites will die before Cochise does realize it? Oh no, what a stupid question. Of course it doesn't. All you care about is yourself and money.'

'Tut, tut, Jarrod, you really shouldn't speak to me like that. These Indians are my friends.'

By now they had almost reached the Indians. Leaving the others, Bull went forward and spoke to Cochise, pointing at the two prisoners, at Phillips and at the wagon. Cochise didn't look particularly pleased but, glancing at the other warriors, Jarrod was quite sure they had glints in their eyes: greedy glints, without pity.

At last Cochise spoke. It caused the Indians all round to break into whoops and furious gestures. Bull turned to Phillips and nodded.

'I think Cochise has just agreed we can be tortured to death,' Evan said miserably.

Cochise spoke again. While some of the Indians led the horses, which were the best spoils of all, to the corral, the others converged on Jarrod and Evan. They were elbowed and jostled further into the camp. Someone spat at them. A stone was thrown. Jarrod fell to his knees and rough hands dragged him up, pushing him forward.

Finally they were shoved into a wickiup. The flap was shut behind them and they were left alone. It was dark and smelly inside, the only light coming from a small opening at the top, designed to let out smoke. In one corner were some old robes and pots and pans.

'God, Jarrod, I'm so scared.' Evan sank down on the ground, leaning against the brush wall.

'You're not the only one.'

'What are they going to do to us?'

'What do you think? Seeing us dead is probably part of Harry's deal for the guns. Damn him to hell and back. All this trouble is caused by his greed.'

'I reckon they'll make us wait, get us real terrified first.'

'I suppose there's no chance of your cap'n finding us before they get round to whatever they plan to do?' Jarrod would now have been more than happy to see the bluecoat soldiers.

'I don't think we can rely on it. Jarrod, did you see any sign of Hazel?'

Jarrod shook his head. 'All I saw were Indians.'

The two young men fell silent. There wasn't much to say. It was quiet outside and Jarrod imagined that somewhere in another hut Cochise and Harry were wrangling over the price of the guns Phillips had to sell. Once he tried opening the flap to look outside but an Apache standing there made a threatening movement with a knife and Jarrod sank back.

After a couple of hours or so, the flap opened and an old woman with grey braids and wrinkled skin came in, accompanied by Young Moon. She carried a waterpouch and a couple of plates of some sort of stew, which she put on the ground in front of them.

The water was warm and tasted alkaline but Jarrod, whose mouth and throat were parched dry, thought water had never tasted so good. Evan was looking at the food.

'What do you think this is? I've heard Indians eat dog.'

'I didn't see any dogs around the camp.'

'Perhaps that's because they've eaten them all.'

'I shouldn't worry. I guess it's lucky we're being given any food at all.'

Slowly the minutes dragged by and became hours and the hours turned into darkness. From outside they could hear speeches being made in low guttural voices, interspersed with cries of joy.

'Never let it be said the Apaches are a stern race with no sense of humour,' Evan said moodily. 'Not when they can celebrate both our demise and the demise of the white man in general.'

Later still came the sounds of celebration; the beating of a drum, whooping and singing. And at the height of excitement, Harry Phillips, accompanied by Bull and Young Moon, came into the wickiup.

'Time to go,' Phillips said happily. 'I'm pleased

to say that the Indians have seen my side of things. With you two dead there'll be no one to identify me as the gun trader.'

'Captain Lambert knows already,' Jarrod said.

'He hasn't got any proof. Now get up and come outside. I'm going to enjoy this. One word of advice, try not to scream. The Indians will respect you more and may make your deaths a bit easier. Scream and they'll hold you in contempt and prolong it even more.'

Outside the whole tribe had gathered in the high moonlight. On seeing the two white men they started to yell and dance in excited anticipation.

Buffeted round heads and bodies, prodded with knives and hit with warclubs, Jarrod and Evan were manhandled through the Indians on their way to the far side of the camp. Here a fire blazed brightly. By it two stakes were set in the ground. Chest high another stake crossed each.

Jarrod stared into the face of one of the bucks. He wasn't very old. Grinning with pleasure, he grabbed Jarrod by the hair and shoved him up against the stake, then hands dragged his arms to the crossbar. Soon he and Evan were tied up. The Indians could do whatever they liked and they were powerless to resist.

'Oh Christ,' moaned Evan. 'There's no way I'm not going to scream. Oh Christ.'

Jarrod looked at him hard. 'Remember you're a lieutenant in the United States Army. Don't let yourself down.'

'Good advice,' Phillips sneered from Jarrod's

side. 'You might remember you were also a lieutenant, in the Confederate States Army. Don't let the South down. Still it ain't you my friends are going to torture right now. It's the Yank over there. You're going to watch. It'll take a long time because they're in the mood for some fun. He won't be killed yet. He should last until round about noon tomorrow. After he's dead, they're going to tie you down over an anthill. I hear tell that's a most painful and long drawn out way to die. After a while you'll be begging for me to shoot you and put you out of your misery. Maybe, Jarrod, if I'm in a good mood I might do so.'

'You know you're one real sonofabitch.'

Harry laughed. 'Nice of you to say so.'

'Go to hell.'

'Oh I believe you'll be going there before me. Ah, the fun is about to begin.' And Phillips stepped back into the shadows.

SEVENTEEN

The Indians sat cross-legged on the ground, in a circle round the stakes. The women and children were behind them, watching from the shadows.

Jarrod shivered as he looked at their expectant faces. Four or five young men, including Bull and Young Moon, gathered in front of Evan. Jarrod had to admire his friend. Evan must have been dreadfully scared but you'd never have known it from the way he stared into the faces of his tormentors.

He was stripped down to his underpants, his clothes and boots being distributed amongst those watching, and then they began.

A twig was pulled from the fire and laid momentarily against his flesh. The shock was so bad Evan couldn't prevent himself groaning aloud. All the Indians stirred and looked at one another.

'Don't give 'em the satisfaction,' Jarrod called across and was slapped around the head to warn him to keep quiet.

For what seemed like a dreadfully long time,

140

Evan hung on the stake while the Apaches tortured him. He was burnt again and again. Another Indian used his knife to cut small pieces of skin from him. It was all delicately done, to ensure the most pain inflicted in the longest possible time.

Once or twice Evan cried out, then quickly clamped his lips together, as if to prevent any sound escaping. Whenever that happened, the Indians showed their appreciation of the torturers' skills. The camp was filled with the awful smell of burnt flesh.

Evan shook his head from side to side in his efforts not to scream, but whatever he did, he couldn't get away from the pain coursing through his body. And eventually he could stand it no longer. He threw his head back and howled out his pain and anguish. Then suddenly he was quiet. Satisfied for the moment, the Indians gave up their tortures and left him alone.

Despite what Phillips had said, Jarrod feared they were going to start on him but slowly the Apaches, their bloodlust over, got up and wandered away. He and Evan were left alone with the dying embers of the fire for company.

'Evan, Evan.'

There was no reply. Jarrod couldn't be sure but he thought that Evan must have fainted or perhaps he was already dead. Now he was alone, Jarrod tried to free himself but he'd been tied too tightly and efficiently. His head ached from where he'd been hit and he was very cold, very scared and suddenly very tired. Despite his efforts not to, his eyes began to close. He was falling into a nightmarish sleep when he felt someone fumbling with the ropes around his wrists.

'What!' he jerked awake, heart beating wildly. 'Who is it?'

'Hush,' a girl's voice said. 'Quiet or someone will hear. It's me, Hazel.'

'Oh thank Christ,' Jarrod sobbed with relief. It wasn't long before the girl had him free. He stumbled on legs that suddenly wouldn't hold him up.

There was still enough light from the fire for him to make out her features. She looked oh so different to the competent neat young nurse who'd looked after him. Her hair fell in tangled straggles down her back and there were several bruises on her face. She was dressed in a too big pair of moccasins and a long buckskin dress that reached her ankles.

Thankful to see her, not only was she alive but she'd saved him from certain death, he hugged her close and she clung to him crying.

'Are you all right? They didn't hurt you?'

'No,' Hazel replied firmly. 'They haven't touched me.'

Jarrod didn't believe her. He was quite certain that the Indians had raped her, probably several times over, at least on the trail, if not here in the village, where maybe she had only been used as a slave. But if that was the fiction she wanted to tell to keep her sanity, then who was he to deny it?

Evan Griffiths was enough in love with her to also pretend she was telling the truth.

Evan! That was if he was still alive.

Taking from Hazel the knife she had used to cut him free, Jarrod went over to where Evan hung, limp and unconscious, on the stake.

'Is he all right?' Hazel asked from by his side.

'I don't know.'

'They made me watch what they did to him. They made me watch what they did to the Fentons and poor Trooper Donnolly.' Hazel put her hands to her face as if to shut out the dreadful images she was carrying around with her. 'It was awful. I can still hear their voices.'

Jarrod didn't know whose voices she meant; the Indians,' the Fentons', or her own. What he did know was that there wasn't enough time to allow her to give into understandable hysterics. He touched her arm, trying to comfort her, and said, 'Don't worry. It's all right now.' Or at least he hoped it was.

When Jarrod had got Evan lying on the ground he could see a faint rise and fall in the young man's chest, and his eyes fluttered once. He could also see that Evan's chest and arms were covered with burn marks and cuts and the wound where he'd been shot was bleeding again. 'The bastards.'

'We must go,' Hazel urged, as anxious as Jarrod to get away.

'Yes, I know. But we'll have to take some things with us. We can't cross the desert without food and water. And horses. And I want a gun. How long do you think we've got until the Indians are about again?'

'Three or four hours at least. Maybe longer. They were all drunk on tiswin last night. And they think themselves so safe in the mountains there aren't any guards posted.'

'What about Harry? The white man who brought us here?'

'He was drunk too. He went to sleep it off by his wagon.'

'Can you get some food and water?'

Hazel nodded.

'When you have, come back and stay with Evan. Keep him quiet. I'll be as quick as I can. And be careful.'

Telling himself to calm down and take it easy, he had plenty of time, Jarrod went first to the corral. His and Evan's horses stood out amongst the other poorly looked after ponies. The saddles and bridles hung as useless prizes on the brush wall lining the corral.

'Here boy,' Jarrod called softly to his horse, which made a small nickering noise in reply and came up to him. Quickly Jarrod saddled and bridled it. Evan's horse was skittish and he was anxious that it didn't get amongst the Indian ponies and make them nervous too. At the third attempt he caught hold of its mane and flung the saddle over its back with the other hand. 'Good boy, good.'

Once that was done the horse quietened down and Jarrod led both animals to the corral gate near to where Evan lay. He left them with their bridles trailing so they wouldn't move away.

Then he started to tiptoe round the camp. Hazel was right. The Indians were drunk. All he could hear were snores and grunts. Still Jarrod was as quiet and careful as he could be, his heart hammering, mouth dry with fear.

He debated whether or not to worry about his saddle-bags. Fear made him want to forget them, to just go, but they contained all he owned. Precious little, in fact, but otherwise he only had what he stood up in. Anyway they should be no problem to retrieve. They had been thrown into the wickiup where he and Evan were earlier kept prisoner.

Jarrod was taken aback when he went inside to find a couple of Indians asleep. But as they were snoring their heads off, he decided it was safe enough to collect the saddle-bags.

Now for a gun. He had to be quick. He'd taken too long as it was.

He looked longingly at Phillips' wagon. It would be just retribution to steal from Harry. He didn't dare.

Slinging the saddle-bags over his shoulder, he crept back up through the village. Then as he was passing a wickiup the flap was pushed back and Cochise emerged to stand in front of him.

'Oh shit,' Jarrod muttered and took a stumbling step backwards, standing rigid with fright.

Without a flicker of emotion the Indian held out a couple of rifles and a revolver towards Jarrod.

Puzzled, scared, Jarrod took them.

'Go.'

Jarrod could only imagine that Cochise was wiser than Harry considered him. That he knew only too well the futility of continuing with the path of fighting. Whatever the reason, Jarrod wasn't going to ponder the problem with him or look his help in the mouth. He went.

Hazel was kneeling on the ground, Evan's head in her lap. 'You've been quick.'

God. It had seemed to Jarrod that he'd been wondering around the village for hours.

'Can you ride behind Evan and support him while I lead the way?'

'Yes.'

Evan's eyes flickered open and he smiled. 'I'm all right.'

'Yeah you look it.' Jarrod grinned back, relief flooding through him that Evan was alive and conscious. 'Come on, if you're so well, you can help us.'

Together Jarrod and Hazel got Evan to his feet. He groaned softly as they helped him on his horse, where, bent low over the animal's neck, he clung to its mane. Jarrod helped Hazel up behind him and she put her arms round the lieutenant supporting him as she took hold of the reins.

Jarrod mounted his own horse and, sticking the revolver in his belt, he put one rifle in the scabbard, holding the other across his knees, and jigged it forward. He thought about stampeding the Indians' ponies but that would only alert some

of the less drunk and might get them shot. All he
wanted to do was get away.

Slowly, as quietly as possible, they rode through
the sleeping village, passed Harry's wagon and
started down the mountainside.

Jarrod glanced back once. It seemed he saw the
figure of Cochise outlined against the waning
moon but he might have been mistaken.

EIGHTEEN

Harry Phillips was in a towering rage. He couldn't believe his bleary, hung-over eyes when he saw the stakes were empty.

'What the hell do you mean they've escaped? How the hell could that happen? You goddamned idiots!'

He strode round the camp yelling at everyone he met, even though they couldn't understand him. Most of the Apaches wisely kept out of his way. His temper was made even worse when he discovered from Bull and Young Moon that Cochise had no intention of sending anyone out after the prisoners.

'Why the goddamn hell not? What's the matter with him? They get back to the fort and tell what they know not only will the soldiers stop me from selling him guns, they'll come after him for what some of his warriors did to the Fentons.'

Bull shrugged and said that the Indians who did that, didn't belong to Cochise's tribe.

'Do you think the goddamned army will care about that? They'll want revenge and it won't matter to them who they get it from.'

'Cochise believes he can persuade the bluecoats that he's innocent.'

'How? By handing over those responsible?'

'Maybe.'

Phillips picked up the warning in Bull's voice. In handing over those responsible Cochise might even take it into his head to hand over the renegade white trader who sold them the guns which made it possible for them to carry out their raids in the first place. Maybe. Maybe in that case it was time to call it quits and leave.

While Phillips could easily leave, there was no way he could call it quits. Not with that bastard Kilkline out there, having got the better of him yet again. No one did that.

'Leave the wagon,' he ordered Bull and Young Moon. 'We're going after 'em ourselves. See if you can persuade some of the others to come as well, whether Cochise likes it or not.'

The two young Indians smiled cruelly at one another. Phillips might be an unpredictable, foul-mouthed white man but he sure did provide excitement.

Throughout the night, Jarrod set as fast a pace as he felt Hazel and Evan could take and as the tricky terrain allowed. The mountain slope was littered with rocks and boulders, tangles of undergrowth and treacherous holes. Here and there they crossed a fast running stream. And he didn't know where they were. All he knew was that they had to go down. With the first light of dawn he saw they were still in the mountains but headed in the right direction, east, towards the rising sun. He kept a grasp on the rifle, eyes forever searching his surroundings.

Despite the help given by Cochise, he feared that the chief wouldn't be able to stop some of the young bucks in the tribe coming after them. And there was Harry as well. Harry wanted him dead and Harry had with him two Indians who presumably knew these mountains. He didn't bother to try and hide their tracks. That would only waste their precious time for Apaches were expert trackers and wouldn't be fooled by anything he tried to do.

Wanting only to get to the valley as quickly as possible, where hopefully the army would be out looking for them, Jarrod made them keep going until it was full light. He came to a halt where an outcropping of rock gave some protection.

'How's Evan?' he asked, helping the lieutenant off the horse.

Hazel raised a tired head, the bruises on her face standing out lividly. 'He's been sleeping.'

'Good, that's probably best.' Jarrod reached into the saddle-bag and brought over his one remaining stolen shirt. 'This will protect him a bit from the sun. I wish there was something we could do for him. We haven't even got that much water we can bathe the burns, we need it to drink.'

'I'm not that good a nurse to know what to do anyway.' Hazel poured some water over her fingers and wet Evan's lips. He moaned once or twice and then opened his eyes. 'How far do you think it is back to the fort?'

'I don't know for sure. Evan and I rode for several days across the desert and then we were a couple more days in Harry's wagon climbing the mountains. What about you? You got any idea?'

Hazel shook her head. 'I was too scared to take any notice of my surroundings.'

'We'd better get on.'

'Oh, can't Evan rest a while longer?'

'I'm afraid not. Our only hope is in outpacing the Apaches.'

Evan had been listening to this exchange and now he said, 'Jarrod, why don't you leave me here and you and Hazel go on and get help? I'll only slow you down and I'll be all right if you hide me.'

'No!' Hazel cried.

For a moment Jarrod was tempted. It made sense. And it would mean safety for him and the girl. But supposing the Indians found Evan before help could arrive? God only knew what they'd do to him. 'No, it's best if we stick together. We stand more of a chance that way. Can you shoot?'

'If I have to.'

'Good,' and Jarrod passed him one of the rifles.

As she mounted behind Evan and hugged him close to her, Hazel looked back. 'I wonder how far behind us they are.'

This time if the Indians caught up and the situation became desperate, she wouldn't hesitate to shoot herself as she had hesitated for that second at the Fentons. Then it had been too late and the Apaches had swarmed into the house and swarmed all over her, and everyone else. What had happened after that she had locked away in part of her memory where she didn't want to think about it. But she knew it would be always be with her, haunting her dreams when she least expected it.

She had feared rescue would never come and had been resigned to being a slave to the spiteful Indian women in Cochise's camp. Then Evan had arrived! She felt like crying as she thought of how courageous he'd been to come searching for her, and of how he'd suffered because of it.

Evan spent the ride slipping in and out of sleep. In one of his more lucid moments, he said to Hazel, 'You're really brave.'

Jarrod thought she was too, for she made no murmur at the pace, drank hardly any water and cared attentively for Evan, holding him, comforting him.

'No, I'm not, I'm terrified.'

'This is neither the time nor the place to say so, Hazel, but I love you and did from the moment I saw you.'

Hazel's eyes filled again with ready tears. 'Don't say that, please. How can you love me after all that has happened?'

'It makes no difference.'

'Yes, it does. I should have listened to you, Evan. Although I knew you were right I went ahead out of stubborn pride. All that happened is my fault.'

'That's strange,' Jarrod said, riding up by her.

'Evan keeps saying it's all his fault. I guess these things happen and it's not much good blaming anyone. You acted out of the best intentions, Hazel, to try and cure a little boy.'

'And me?' Evan asked.

'Well, I guess you acted out of inexperience. And if McPhee hadn't been busted back to private for what he did to me he maybe would have been there to stop you both. So you could say it was all my fault.'

Hazel smiled, for the first time in what seemed to her like a very very long time. She reached round, gripping Evan's hand tightly, telling him without words that she loved him too. 'I daresay when we get back to the fort you'll be in too much trouble with Captain Lambert and I'll be in too much trouble with Papa for either of us to think about blaming one another.'

Jarrod smiled as well, glad to see that the girl hadn't lost her sense of humour; that was the best way to recovery.

Round about mid-afternoon, they were crossing a small meadow when Jarrod heard Hazel scream. Turning in his saddle he saw Bull and Young Moon charging down the hill towards them. There were two other Indians with them. Several shots rang out!

NINETEEN

If he'd been on his own, Jarrod would have made a run for it, trusting not so much to his superior skills on horseback, but at least on his superior horse, and his better marksmanship. Even if Hazel could ride as well as him, there was no way that Evan could put up with that sort of punishment. They had to make a stand for it, here, in the middle of the meadow.

'Dismount, dismount!' he yelled. Getting off his horse he pulled Evan roughly to the ground and tossed the reins of both animals at Hazel. 'Get the horses to the rear. Hold them so they don't run off.'

Scared Hazel did as she was told.

'Evan, make sure you've got something to hit before you fire. We haven't got that much ammunition.'

Jarrod went down on one knee and levered off a shot at the Indian in the lead. The Indian and his horse went down in a flurry and while the horse got up, the Indian didn't.

'Can you see Phillips?'

'Harry's no fool,' Jarrod said bitterly. 'He likes the odds distinctly in his favour. He won't risk getting shot but he'll want to be around at the end. But we're not going to provide him with the sort of ending he wants, not that easily anyway.'

Time and time again the three remaining Indians charged, always swerving away before getting too close, trying to draw their fire. The defenders were well and truly pinned down on the mountainside, unable to ride away, risking getting shot if they stayed. The Indians were triumphant, believing they had the upper hand.

Suddenly Jarrod gave a grunt of pain and fell sideways, clutching at his leg.

'What's the matter?' Evan cried.

An arrow was sticking out of Jarrod's leg. He lay on his side, moaning. It hurt like hell.

It was the signal for an attack. For seeing one of the two white men down and out of it, the Apaches meant business.

'Here they come!' Hazel screamed.

'Hazel!' Evan fumbled for Jarrod's revolver, somehow got hold of it and threw it at the girl.

She caught it, cocked it and aiming, fired, the recoil almost knocking her off her feet.

Bull was on top of them, mouth open in a scream, that Evan couldn't hear. Evan raised the rifle and pressed the trigger. The bullet slammed into Bull's chest and, as if he had crashed into a wall he somersaulted from his horse and bounced along the ground, before coming to a halt by Evan's elbow.

Evan didn't get the chance for another shot. Young Moon bore down on him. From his horse, he slammed Evan in the side of the head with his warclub, knocking him out. Leaping from his horse, the Indian drew his knife, clutching at Evan's hair, pulling his head up, howling in triumph.

Meanwhile Hazel forgetting all about shooting herself had discharged her last bullet at the remaining Indian, who, unhit, galloped by, before turning his horse intending to charge again. 'Jarrod, Jarrod!' she screamed.

Through the pain fogging his mind, Jarrod knew he had to do something or they were all going to die. Frantically, he grabbed for the rifle he'd dropped. And just as Young Moon was about to scalp Evan, he shot the Indian.

Young Moon's yells of triumph changed to one of pain. He jerked round, raised his knife as if to throw it at Jarrod, and Jarrod shot him again. This time the bullet smashed into the Indian's skull and in a blossom of blood and brains he collapsed on the ground.

No longer liking the odds, the third Indian decided to quit and rode from the scene of the battle as fast as he could.

'It's over, over,' Hazel whispered.

'Not until I find out about Harry. He might still be around. He could have some more Indians with him. I'll have to go and see.'

'But you're wounded.'

'You'll have to pull the arrow out.'

'I can't.'

'Yes, you can. Come on, you're meant to be a nurse.'

Gritting her teeth, half closing her eyes, Hazel gripped the arrow.

'Pull!'

And she did. Jarrod screamed and collapsed on his back, panting, as Hazel quickly wrapped a piece of his shirt round the wound.

'You shouldn't move,' she objected anxiously.

'I must. I've got to make sure we're safe.'

With Hazel's help, Jarrod got to his feet and hobbled over to his horse. He was scared, wondering if he was now going to limp in both legs. Once in the saddle, he felt slightly better. Cautiously he rode back across the meadow to the spot where the Indians had appeared. The third Indian was lying there dead. Maybe Hazel had shot him but it would have been just like Harry to shoot someone who had become a nuisance.

But of Harry himself there was no sign. Had he been with the Indians? Or had he remained at Cochise's camp? Whatever the answer, Jarrod was sure he wouldn't face them on his own.

Slowly he rode back to where Hazel waited.

'Now you've got two invalids on your hands,' Jarrod said, and falling to his knees on the ground, was first violently sick and then fainted.

Three days later they were in the foothills.

Jarrod's leg hurt him but unlike when he got shot there seemed to be no permanent damage and already the pain was lessening. He began to make plans.

Maybe he could see Evan and Hazel across the

desert and then if Evan was better leave them.
Evan was still suffering the effects of the Indians'
torture and he had a nasty head wound, but he
was holding on, and with Hazel to help him could
travel quite well.

Certainly Jarrod didn't want to get anywhere
near the fort. That would be to risk recapture and
be in just as bad a position as before. Evan and
Hazel would understand. They had each other.

But Jarrod didn't have time to put his plans
into practice. Because the next day they met the
army patrol led by Sergeant McPhee.

Jarrod could do nothing but come to a halt as the
soldiers surrounded them all. Several of the troopers recognized him and pulled out their guns.

'What's going on here?' McPhee demanded. 'My
God, Lieutenant!'

'He's been tortured.'

'I can see that! Help him some of you.'

'I'm all right,' Evan said in as dignified voice as
he could manage. He was helped from his horse
and laid gently on the ground.

Looking as if she was going to cry, Hazel went
to crouch by him, holding his hand. It was as if she
never wanted to let him go.

'Miss Dunlop we were all so worried about you.
Thank Christ we found you.'

'McPhee, I see you're a sergeant again,' Evan
spoke from where a couple of the troopers were
somewhat ineffectually bathing his wounds.

'Yes, Lieutenant.'

'Well if you want to remain one, you will not

hurt this man again. He saved my life, when he had no need to. Without him both Hazel, Miss Dunlop, and I would be dead.'

'He's right. Please, Mr McPhee, tell the men to put their guns away.'

Jarrod watched all this anxiously. Would McPhee do what they wanted or would he be inclined to beat him up again, or have him shot?

McPhee was no fool. He could work out for himself something of what happened. Lieutenant Griffiths had naturally gotten himself into a scrape, which didn't surprise him in the least. And somehow and for some reason Mr Jarrod Kilkline had helped him out of it. McPhee had little respect for most of his superior officers, but at the same time, imbued with army discipline, he felt their needs and wants came first. Kilkline deserved something for what he had done.

While his instincts were to take Kilkline back to the fort, sometimes, much to his own surprise, he acted in a manner completely alien to his character. This was one such occasion.

'Mr Kilkline you're free to go. But,' he pointed a finger at him, 'if I ever see you again, I'll carry on where I left off. Understand?'

'Yeah, sure.'

'What's this?' A voice demanded and someone rode through the circle of troopers.

Startled, Jarrod recognized the weedy man who'd been at the start of all his current troubles.

'Sergeant, that man is a wanted stagecoach robber. You can't let him go. I demand that you hold him.'

'I'm sorry. He helped the lieutenant there and Miss Dunlop.'

'Do you think I care about that?' Peabody went to draw one of his hidden guns.

'Stop him,' Evan cried.

'No, Mr Peabody, don't.' McPhee pulled his own pistol and pointed it at Peabody's nose. 'He goes free. Go on Kilkline, get outa here.'

Jarrod needed no second bidding. He didn't know who this Peabody was but if he'd been on his trail all this time he was obviously someone to be reckoned with. He didn't want to give McPhee the chance to change his mind either. He glanced at Evan and Hazel and grinned. 'See you sometime.'

'I hope so, Jarrod,' Evan raised a hand in farewell.

'I'll never forget you,' Hazel ran up to him and took his hands in hers, gripping them for a long moment.

Jarrod put spurs to his horse and galloped away, it seemed he was always saying goodbye. At the top of the hill he paused to glance back but already the figures were tiny as if they were unreal toys.

Angrily Peabody turned to McPhee. 'You fool! You haven't heard the last of this!'

'Tell me about it,' McPhee said with a shrug.

Peabody looked at Jarrod's diminishing figure. 'And nor have you, Mr Jarrod Kilkline, nor have you.'